CORPSMAN!

*"He who sheds his blood with me
this day is my brother."*
—Shakespeare

Bruce Littell

PublishAmerica
Baltimore

© 2008 by Bruce Littell.
All rights reserved. No part of this book may be reproduced, stored in a retrieval system or transmitted in any form or by any means without the prior written permission of the publishers, except by a reviewer who may quote brief passages in a review to be printed in a newspaper, magazine or journal.

First printing

This is a work of fiction. Names, characters, places, and incidents either are the product of the author's imagination or are used fictitiously. Any resemblance to actual persons, living or dead, events, or locales is entirely coincidental

ISBN: 1-60672-655-2
PUBLISHED BY PUBLISHAMERICA, LLLP
www.publishamerica.com
Baltimore

Printed in the United States of America

This one's for Joshua

*Dedicated to the memory of Eugene B. Sledge
November 4, 1923–March 3, 2001*

Acknowledgments

Materials upon which I have drawn, and borrowed unashamedly include:

With the Old Breed by E.B. Sledge, Presidio Press, 1981.

Utmost Savagery: The Three Days of Tarawa, by Colonel Joseph H. Alexander, Random House, 1995.

Hell Looks Different Now, by J. "Doc" Mc Niff, Protea Publishing, 2001.

Brotherhood of Heroes, by Bill Sloan, Simon and Schuster, 2005.

Fields of Fire, by James Webb. Simon and Schuster, 1978.

One Square Mile of Hell, by John Wukovits, Penguin Books Ltd., 2006.

Various sources on the internet.

Preface

Unlike the Army, whose medical personnel were supplied from its own ranks, the Navy supplied medical personnel to the Marines. Many of the Navy corpsmen performed their duties on board hospital ships, but the most important were those at the front lines, or on the beach evacuation stations. The corpsmen were familiar with the amphibious island warfare that the Marines used in the Pacific Theater of WWII. These men first received medical training in naval hospitals, but then moved on to Marine bases to finish their instructions as corpsmen. They trained under the same conditions as the men they would treat.

The first relationship between the Hospital Corps and the U.S. Marines was established in 1898, when hospital corpsmen were assigned to the Marine Corps Expeditionary Battalion, which landed at Guantanamo Bay during the Spanish-American War.

In the summer of 1902, the first Hospital Corps Training School was opened at the Naval Hospital in Portsmouth, Virginia. The purpose of the school was to provide uniform and systematic training for the new personnel entering the Hospital Corps. Many graduates of this school saw their first duty under fire with the Marines at Haiti.

During WWII hospital corpsmen served virtually on every front. Corpsmen were at the forefront of every invasion. They were involved in every action at sea. A total of 889 corpsmen were mortally wounded. Others died heroically from diseases they were trying to combat. In all the Corps casualty list contains 1724 names. During WWII, 7 hospital corpsmen received the Medal of Honor, 67 received Navy Crosses, and 464 received Silver Stars. As stated by Secretary of the Navy James Forrestal in 1945, "The hospital corpsmen saved lives on all beaches that the Marines stormed.... You corpsmen performed foxhole surgery while shell fragments clipped your clothing, shattered the plasma bottles from which you poured new life into the wounded, and sniper's bullets were aimed at the brassards on your arms." No other individual corps, before or since has been so singled out and honored.

1
McCamey, Texas, 1940

Thad Hayes had just graduated from McCamey High School, and was working that summer, as he had the previous two summers for Dr. Orville Sweet, the town's only veterinarian. Doc Sweet needed someone to mind the clinic while he was out treating livestock, even though there wasn't a whole lot of livestock to treat. But it was a good excuse to leave the clinic so that he could hang out at the pool hall, knock down a Schlitz (the beer that made Milwaukee famous) or two, or three, play snooker, and tell lies with the rest of the old timers.

Thad's plan was to attend Texas A&M in the fall and study veterinary medicine, and he knew that his experience working for Dr. Sweet could only help. He assisted with surgeries and the routine treatment of cats, dogs, and one parakeet, as well as cleaning the cages and mopping the floors before going home at night. About that parakeet: seems the guy's wife was out of town and had left her much loved parakeet in care of her husband. Tweety got out of her cage, flew into a closed window, and the poor guy was afraid that the bird had broken its neck. He panicked, brought the parakeet to Dr. Sweet, telling him that if the bird died, he was as good as dead. Dr. Sweet massaged the bird's neck. Bird lived. Guy lived. End of story.

McCamey was a West Texas town fifty miles south of Odessa. In 1925 oil was discovered, and almost overnight, the population grew from very few to 10,000. Then in 1928 Shell Oil Company built a huge oil-storage reservoir, designed to hold one million barrels of oil. It leaked. Besides that, the oil was playing out, and most of the good citizens decided to seek their fortunes elsewhere. The population in 1940 was 2600.

Thad was born in 1922 in Midland, where his dad was a pharmacist. Mr. Hayes saw opportunity in McCamey, so along with his mother and older sister Josie, they moved in 1926, and Mr. Hayes became the proud owner of the Rexall Drugstore, writing prescriptions and passing out medications for dinged-up oil-field workers, as well as tending the soda fountain until he could afford a soda jerk. The drugstore was across the street from the school. Elementary, junior high, and the high school all lumped together, and the drugstore was a popular after-school hang-out. Lots of cherry cokes. A soda jerk was eventually hired, and at times Thad would have to fill in for him, sweep the floor, straighten the magazine rack. Every once in awhile, his daddy would give him a quarter for his efforts, but most of the time he told him was working for room and board.

All through school Thad was no more than an average student. He played the usual sports, excelling in none. Had the same girl friend, Lou Ann, all through junior high and high school. They weren't exactly going steady but very seldom dated anyone else. Never talked about getting married but both assumed that it would happen.

However, one Saturday afternoon while Thad was working at the vet clinic, Linda Firestone brought in her cat for a spay job. A few days earlier an older woman had left her pet monkey, said she was going to be traveling to Europe, couldn't take the monkey, and wanted the little fellow put to sleep. Thad asked her if he couldn't keep him instead. She agreed.

Anyhow, Linda Firestone was in Thad's class. She was Head Cheerleader, Most Beautiful Girl, Most Popular and Most Everything Else. He saw this as his opportunity to put a move on Miss Everything. While he was putting the cat in a cage, awaiting Dr. Sweet's magic, he asked her if she would like to see his monkey.

"What?"

He told her he had a pet monkey. Would she like to see it?

She said, "Sure," so he went and fetched said monkey from his cage, sat him on his shoulder, and returned to the reception area where Linda was waiting.

She said, "How cute," and reached for him.

The critter bit Thad on the ear, peed down his neck, and then jumped up on a curtain rod over the window. So much for impressing Miss Everything. He soon found another taker for the little guy, all the while hoping that he hadn't been bitten by a rabid monkey.

The night before Thad left for A&M, he took Lou Ann to the movies, a double feature: *The Invisible Man Returns* and *The Mummy's Hand*. Afterward, in Mr. Hayes' black 1939 Buick, the model with spare-tire mounts on the front fenders, a gangster car, they parked at their usual spot, on a hill overlooking about a hundred oilfield flares. Lou Ann said it reminded her of a big ballroom. Lighted cigarettes.

After the usual bout of kissing, hugging, groping, and

fumbling around, they talked. Thad's dad would drive him to College Station in the morning, see to it that he got enrolled. He told Lou Ann that he would be home for Christmas and that he would be sure to bring her something from the A&M gift shop. Lou Ann had just finished her junior year and planned to go to Texas Women's University and study elementary education. Dr. Thadius Hayes, Veterinarian, and Mrs. Lou Ann Hayes, school marm. Perfect. She said she would rather go to A&M, but since A&M was an all male, military institution, that was pretty much out of the question. Also said that she would wait. Wouldn't date anyone else. Thad told her that he wouldn't either. No problem there.

If Thad would have had a choice, another college where he could study veterinary medicine, he would have jumped all over it. A&M, a military school, was the only Texas college to offer Veterinary Medicine, and he couldn't imagine going out of state, so A&M it was. It was the military that he would have preferred to avoid. By nature he was a headstrong boy and didn't take orders well, and the thought of wearing a uniform every day instead of boots and jeans didn't sit well at all.

Having put all that aside, the morning after he and Lou Ann said their goodbyes, he kissed his mother goodbye, hugged Josie, he and Mr. Hayes climbed into the Buick, and they were gone. Seven hours, more or less to College Station.

While stopping for lunch in Lampasas, over chicken fried steaks and french fries, Mr. Hayes told Thad how he would have liked to have served in The Great War, but he was unable to because of his disability. One leg was an inch and a half shorter than the other. Now, with a built up shoe, the limp was barely noticeable. He went on to say how proud he was of his son going to a military school, where he would graduate as a Second Lieutenant, and if there ever was another war, which at the time seemed pretty darned likely, at least he would go as an officer, hopefully staying out of harm's way.

His first two years at A&M, Thad would be required to be in the Corps of Cadets. Then, if he was accepted into vet school, he would be given the option of staying in the Corps, or joining the civilian ranks. At least he had that to look forward to.

They arrived at the campus later that afternoon, found Thad's dorm, got him settled in, said their goodbyes, and Mr. Hayes hit the road back to McCamey, while Thad was getting acquainted with his new room mate, a boy from Dallas, Robert Bowman. Having never been around too many big-city folk, Thad felt like a bumpkin. In fact, Robert told him he talked like a bumpkin. Thad considered kicking his ass, but Robert assured him he was just kidding. Robert, "Call me Bob," apologized, and they later went off to the mess hall where they were joined by several thousand soon-to-be Texas Aggies.

Registration the next day went off without a hitch. They were issued their uniforms and bought their books. Later were ordered to fall out, get into formation on the street in front of the dorm, and Thad got a look at the rest of his dorm mates, Battery Seven, Field Artillery. They marched to evening chow, afterwards did a little close-order drill, then had meetings with their upper classmen.

First day of classes they went to English, algebra and chemistry. Next day it was zoology and military science. Somewhat overwhelmed, Thad dug in. He spent more time studying than he ever did at McCamey High, and still struggled. His grades that first semester were average at best. If he had any hope of getting accepted into vet school he was going to have to turn it up a notch. Meanwhile, Bob, majoring in civil engineering, was knocking down As and Bs with seemingly a minimum of effort. This set Thad to thinking that life wasn't fair. Might have to kick big city boy Bob's ass.

That fall brought football games, Corps trips, and home for Christmas vacation. He groped and fumbled with Lou Ann and tried to explain to Mr. Hayes that even though his grades weren't all that good, he was sure that they would improve dramatically the next semester.

However, the next semester was more of the same. Average grades weren't good enough. Then, his sophomore year, along came organic chemistry, and that did it. Organic chemistry done him in, pretty well screwed any plans that he may have had about vet school.

He had taken the hazing as a freshman, but then as a sophomore, a junior got on his case about un-shined shoes, brass in need of polishing, told him he was a disgrace to the Corps, and should go back to Dog Patch where he came from. Thad stood at attention, listened to what the junior had to say, then punched him out, and spent the next six weeks confined to his dorm, except for classes and meals.

He returned home following his sophomore year, but this summer, rather than working for Dr. Sweet, he went to work for Shell Pipe Line as a welder's helper, a swamper on the trucks hauling pipe. One day while laying pipe in Big Lake, he was helping a welder, and had forgotten his protective goggles He'd left them in the truck with the dog house on the back, which carried the crew to and from jobs. No problem. When the welder would strike his arc, Thad would look away, and when the welding stopped, he would turn and hand the welder another rod. That was all well and good, but this particular welder had the habit of stopping his weld even if he didn't need a new rod. Thad would turn to hand him a rod, the welder would strike his arc again, and of course Thad would see the whole thing in living color. After doing this two or three times, he learned to wait till the welder asked for a new rod before turning his head.

Come quitting time, the crew headed back down the line about a half mile to the crew truck. When they got to the truck it was learned that the shovels and grubbing hoe had been left where they had been working, and Thad, being the new guy, was elected to go back and fetch the tools. Which he did. When he returned the crew was gone, the truck was gone, and Thad of the blistered eyes would have to get back to McCamey on his own.

He walked to a pay phone, called Lou Ann, and told her to come and get him. By the time she got there, Thad was sitting on the curb, his eyes were burning. He was irritable, argumentative, an all-around pain in the ass. He threw the tools into the back seat, and Lou Ann put up with him for about twenty miles, and finally pulled over to the side of the road and told him to get out and walk.

He said fine, he'd thumb a ride, and climbed out.

He eventually caught a ride, made it home, and told his daddy that he needed eye drops for his burning eyes. Mr. Hayes assured him that eye drops wouldn't do any good. What he needed was potato juice. He cut up a potato, squeezed some of the juice into a handkerchief and told Thad to put that on his eyes. Not exactly instant relief, but after awhile the pain was gone. "Learn that in pharmacy school?"

"Nope. Welders that come into the drugstore."

"Oh."

The following morning, he reported to work, marched into the pusher's office, dumped two shovels and a grubbing hoe on his desk and told him to go fuck himself.

That night, he and Lou Ann made up. There was more groping on the hill overlooking the giant ballroom.

The Japanese had attacked Pearl Harbor the previous December, and Thad didn't want to be drafted. He decided to enlist. With what little he had learned about the Army after two years in the Cadet Corps, he had made up his mind that it wasn't for him. At the time soldiers were fighting in Europe, sleeping on the ground, eating K rations. Marines were fighting Japs and malaria in the Pacific. The Navy was the way to go. A roof over his head, a bunk to sleep in, and three square meals a day. See the world. Yessiree!

Naturally, his daddy was disappointed, but on that September morning, 1942, they once again climbed into the Buick and drove to Odessa to the Navy recruitment office. Thad raised his right hand, swore to uphold a bunch of stuff, and that's all it took. Right. He was a sailor headed for the Recruit Training Command, Great Lakes, Illinois.

2

While waiting at the Greyhound bus station Thad met another recruit, a boy from Monahans named Bobby Leeds. Bobby claimed to be eighteen, but sure didn't look it. Said he joined the Navy so he wouldn't be drafted into the Army. Later Thad learned that Bobby had been orphaned at the age of four and was raised by an alcoholic, abusive uncle, and of course was anxious to remove himself from the hurtful situation. Besides, he was afraid he had knocked up his girlfriend, so he figured that it was a good time to get out of town, especially since the girl friend's daddy was the sheriff. At every stop Bobby expected the law to be there waiting to arrest him as he got off the bus.

At the bus station Thad bought a *Life Magazine* and the latest copy of *Illustrated Football Annual*, and had brought a book from home, *The Ox-Bow Incident*. The cover of the *Life Magazine* had a picture of a sailor, looking mighty sharp in his white uniform and carrying a rifle. Thad thought *I didn't join the Navy to carry no rifle.*

A&M had won the National Championship a few years earlier, and he was anxious to see if the *Illustrated Football Annual* was giving them a chance to do it again. The magazine claimed it was going to be a race between Notre Dame, Michigan, and Navy.

The Aggies weren't even mentioned in the top twenty. Where have you gone, Jarrin' John Kimbrough?

As the bus rolled on toward Ft. Worth and all points beyond Thad got to know his new pal, Bobby. In fact he got to know more about him than he would have liked. Young Bobby, it seems, was more than a troubled youth. Had he been older, he would have been a convicted felon. Twelve-year-old Bobby and two of his friends, two other "troubled youths," had robbed the town's only filling station, beating the attendant senseless with a tire iron, and getting away with twelve dollars and thirteen cents. They were caught the next day, trying to steal a 1934 Chevrolet, and arrested by the local sheriff, his possibly pregnant girlfriend's father.

The trial lasted less than a half day. The boys were found guilty of robbery, assault, and battery, as well as attempted burglary, and were packed off to reform school. After serving his two-year sentence Bobby returned to Monahans, found he didn't fit in with the rest of the ninth graders, and quit school. He got a job fixing flats and pumping gas at the same Mobilgas station he had robbed only two years earlier.

That night the bus broke down somewhere in the middle of Arkansas. The bus driver said, "Sorry for the inconvenience, folks. Ain't serious. We'll be back on the road in just a little bit." The "little bit" turned into more than an hour while the driver worked on the engine. He finally told the passengers that there was a town just a mile or so up the road. If they wanted to they could walk up there. He knew of a café that was open all night, and he would pick them up as soon as he got the bus running.

Thad and Bobby opted for the walk, found the café, and sat at the counter. Thad ordered a slice of apple pie and coffee, while Bobby went for a cheeseburger and a coke.

After finishing eating Bobby lit a cigarette and offered one to Thad.

"No thanks."

Bobby said, "You see that drug store on the other side of the road just a few blocks back?"

"No, I didn't notice. What about it?"

"Let's rob it. Easy pickin's. In and out in two minutes. What do you say?"

"I say you're out of your freakin' mind."

"Come on, man. It must be close to closing time. Still got all the cash."

"Bobby, this time they won't be talking reform school. You get caught, you're going to prison, man. Huntsville. Think about it. Besides, you need a gun."

"Okay, Puss. Don't wait for me. I'll jump back on the bus as soon as it gets here."

With that being said, young Bobby Leeds was out the door, hands in his pockets, headed toward the drug store.

Thad ordered another cup of coffee, expecting to hear sirens and gunshots at any minute. Maybe the fool did have a gun. Another thirty minutes, and the bus rolled up. He looked back toward the drug store, saw a cop car, but no Bobby.

He climbed back on the bus, expecting Bobby to jump on. It didn't happen. The bus pulled out. Still no Bobby. Thad was thinking, *I wonder if he's AWOL? Probably so, since he's been sworn in. That means the shore patrol will be after him. And then there's Daisy Mae's, or whatever the hell her name is, daddy, the sheriff. He'll surely be looking. There's also the local cops who are upset because he robbed their drug store. Way to go, Bobby. The only players not involved are the F.B.I. Give them time.*

As the bus rolled on, sans Bobby, Thad spent the time sleeping, checking out the countryside, and reading his book, *The Ox-Bow Incident*, about a posse-chasing killers. It reminded him of Bobby's posse, but Bobby wasn't a killer. Not yet, anyhow.

They arrived in Chicago at four in the morning. The driver told Thad that this was the end of the line. He would have to catch another bus for the short ride to Great Lakes. It wasn't long before the Navy bus arrived, loaded up Thad and a few sailors, and headed to the base.

Recruit Training Command, Great Lakes, Illinois. Thad would spend eight weeks here, at boot camp, then hopefully be assigned to a battleship. An aircraft carrier would be nice, or even a destroyer. He would sail off into the sunset, the seven seas, romance, adventure, see the world. Not so fast, Thad.

That first day, after being fed in the huge mess hall, the recruits began processing. Thad sat at a desk, being interviewed by a chief petty officer, holding a folder with the papers Thad had filled out when he enlisted. After his little welcoming speech, he said, "I see here that you worked for a veterinarian, and had two years of pre-vet. That right?"

Thad said, "Yes, sir," wondering what this had to do with anything.

"How would you like to be a corpsman?"

"What's a corpsman?"

"A corpsman is a doctor of sorts. The Naval Hospital Corps. You see, the Army provides medics from within their own ranks, but the Navy supplies the Marine Corps with medical personnel, corpsmen."

"I'd be attached to the Marine Corps?"

"That's about the size of it."

"What if I don't want to?"

"Doesn't matter. You'll volunteer anyhow. Look, it ain't so bad. You might be assigned to a hospital ship. Three hots and a cot and a roof over you head."

"Or?"

"You'll join a Marine unit and stay with them wherever they go."

"You mean like Guadalcanal?"

"Something like that."

"Oh, man. I joined the Navy to avoid that kind of stuff, and I know absolutely nothing about treating humans. All my experience has been taking care of cats and dogs."

"Not to worry. You'll be trained at the Hospital Corps School in San Diego."

"I just got off the bus, and now you're sending me to San Diego?"

"That's about the size of it."

"I don't have any choice, do I?"

"Nope."

The next day Thad was on a train headed for sunny California, thinking he had made a huge mistake. He should have joined the Air Corps.

Thad spent the next fourteen weeks training to become a Navy corpsman, taking classes in anatomy and physiology, pharmacy and toxicology, personnel hygiene, administering first aid, giving shots, blood transfusions, even emergency dental care.

He finished in the top third of his class, still not too thrilled over the thought of serving with marines, but he'd give it his best shot. He was "Doc."

3
Camp Pendleton, California, 1943

Having completed his training in San Diego, and after returning from thirty-day's leave, Pharmacists' Mate Third Class Hayes reported to Camp Pendleton for training with marines. *Here we go*, thought Thad. *I think I screwed up.*

He was processed in and told he was now a member of the First Platoon, Charlie Company, First Battalion, Sixth Marine Regiment, Second Marine Division. He threw his sea bag on a truck, and that afternoon was delivered to his Quonset hut, where he introduced himself to the rest of the platoon. These people would become his family for who knows how long. Most were as green as he was, having graduated from boot camp only a few weeks earlier and had only a vague idea why a sailor was joining their elite ranks. His uniform was just like theirs except for the strange rank insignia on his sleeves.

After the introductions, they were ordered to fall out into the company street, where Thad got his first look at Sergeant Bradley, the company first sergeant. Sergeant Bradley was a tall, rangy guy, maybe an athlete. Then came Lieutenant Stanley, the platoon leader. They made the usual welcoming speeches and then told the men to buckle up their chin straps, because the next six weeks were going to be a bitch.

They were marched to evening chow, then back to the Quonset. Thad got his gear squared away and was joined by his bunk mate, Joe Louis Boyd, a soft-spoken colored boy from Chicago, built like a large safe. When asked the obvious, Joe said that his daddy had hopes for him to become a fighter. Didn't take. Joe Louis Boyd didn't like to fight. When fighting was the only option, always done in the streets, Joe usually destroyed his opponent, but he received no satisfaction whipping up on people. Fortunately, because of his size, he was generally avoided by those looking for a fight, but inevitably, there were those who had to test themselves against this big, black man.

Later, Sergeant Bradley came to the Quonset hut and outlined for them what they could expect in the coming weeks. Lectures, weapons familiarization, field problems, long marches. Any questions? The one called Roy Boy asked what was the plan for them after they completed this six weeks of infantry combat training. The sergeant said he didn't know; it was up to the powers that be, but if it was up to him they'd all jump on a ship and go to the Pacific and kill Japs. Sergeant Bradley might be a little gung ho.

With that he bade them, "Good night, girls; turn off the lights and get some sleep. Tomorrow is going to be a busy day, and you're going to need all the rest you can get."

The following morning began with reveille at 0500. He grabbed a shave at the company head, marched to chow, got the barracks squared away, backed into the company street and marched to the drill field for an hour of calisthenics. Squad leaders and fire-team leaders were appointed, weapons were issued, and the platoon went back to the drill field for some close-order drill. Thad, not having a whole lot of experience with this close-order drill business, marched at the rear of the first squad and couldn't help from screwing up. "Yes, Sergeant, I know my right foot from my left."

"You fucking sailors don't march worth a damn."

At A&M he had close order drill, but nothing like this, and at Hospital Corps School in San Diego, they did have close order drill, but were never too serious about it. What the hell's "oblique?"

The rest of the day was spent listening to lectures, and sitting in bleachers watching demonstrations of various weapons, mortars, light- and heavy-machine guns, and one demonstration, "Why you don't want to try to out run a hand grenade." Fortunately, for Roy Boy, it wasn't a real grenade.

Thus ended day one. They thought. That night, back in the company street, with helmets, packs and weapons, they were told by Sergeant Bradley that they were going to take a walk. No problem. Then the sergeant told them to empty their canteens.

"Say, what? Empty our canteens?"

"You got it. Empty 'em, now."

There was the sound of water being poured from forty canteens into the company street, then right face, right shoulder arms, forward march, and there they went, off, not to see the Wizard, but to become friends with the hills of Camp Pendleton. Pendleton's got lots of hills—more hills than flat places. Then there was the one they called, "Nellie's Tit."

Single file, at a route step, they followed Captain Bartholomew, the Company Commander in the lead. The boys were introduced to the hill, affectionately called Nellie's Tit, first shot out of the box. "Holy mackerel, Saphire! Give us a break."

By the time they got to the top, there were stragglers not even half way up the hill. As they slowly made it to the top, the last, bringing up the rear, was Willis. Willis was overweight, seemed to be a nice kid, but Thad had his doubts about his being around at the end of the six weeks. Captain Bartholomew seemed to be barely winded. Lieutenant Stanley, on the other hand, didn't look too good. He tried to look strong but failed miserably.

They took a ten-minute break, thinking about all the water left on the company street, and they were off again. Fortunately, the night was relatively cool. Otherwise, Thad was sure that their trail would be littered with dead marines, Thad among them. More hills, but none as severe as Nellie's Tit.

After two more hours of humping, men began to fall out. The survivors would be prodded on by Sergeant Bradley and managed to stagger on. All except Willis. Thad passed him laying on the side of the road, seeming to have convulsions. His first thought was to stop and give him some sort of aid, but a weapons carrier, a little four-wheel-drive truck, stopped, loaded Willis into the back where he joined two others that had fallen out. Thad was thinking, *That's a good deal. They're going to try to kill us. Those that don't die will be marines. Semper Fi!*

They finally made it back to their Quonset hut in time for lights out, but first, lined up at the drinking fountain to see if they could drain it. Thad swore that he would never, ever be thirsty again.

In the days that followed, more of the same, but none of the "Empty your canteens" drill. They attacked the obstacle course. Willis had returned to the company appearing to be none the worse for wear. He struggled through the obstacle course but made it. Thad thought, *Maybe there's hope for the boy after all.* Then there was the tower with the rope ladders hanging over the side. It was explained that, "This is how you're going to get from the ship into the landing craft. Keep your hands on the verticals so they don't get stepped on." Some figured it was easier to use the horizontal ropes rather than the verticals. Those that were caught committing this sin, when they reached the ground, had their hands stepped on by Gunnery Sergeant Mancillas. Gunny Mancillas had served in Shanghai with the China Marines, the Old Corps. Seemed like a nice enough guy, but stepping on someone's hands?

During the third week the company was marched, helmets, packs and weapons, to the place called "The Infiltration Course." It was a depression. A muddy depression at least thirty yards across, kept that way by the water truck standing by. Strung across the depression were several strands of barbed wire, two or three feet above the ground, and on one side was a .30 caliber machine gun. Thad figured, *This don't look good at all*, and he was right. It wasn't.

"This is the drill," explained the gunny. "You people," he was always saying, "you people," "will remove your packs, lie on your backs, stay under the barbed wire, and somehow make it to the other side without getting killed. The machine gun will be firing live rounds about a foot or so above your head. If you don't do something stupid, like trying to get up and run, you may make it. Good luck, and bon voyage." Gunny had a sense of humor.

Thad was in the first group. The first few yards, no problem. A little further and the machine gun opened up, short bursts, but pretty damned effective. They sure got his attention, anyhow. He was inching along on his back, in the mud, bullets zinging just above his head, and he was thinking, *It can't get any worse*. Just then it got worse. The explosions. Explosive charges had been placed outside the lanes the marines were struggling through. The first one went off, and Thad was thinking, *Jesus Christ. They could have at least warned us*. He got to the first run of barbed wire, held it up with his rifle, while he wormed his way underneath it. He kept scooting along on his back through the mud, machine gun fire, more barbed wire, more explosions, and finally made it to the other side, where the gunny was waiting. He put his arm around Thad's shoulder and said, "Is this fun, or what?"

After the third week, they got their first weekend liberty. Thad, Davis, a big, raw-boned boy from northern California, and Rat, a would-be gangster from the Bronx, decided to go to L.A., catch a movie, and see what happened after that.

Earlier that summer in Los Angeles was a summer of violence, the Zoot Suit Riots. Drunken military men on their way back to base after a night of carousing were often jumped by civilian minority youth, the zoot suiters, hoping to teach them proper respect. Sailors would often insult Mexican Americans as they traveled through their neighborhood. In the barrios there were rumors of sailors searching out Mexican American girls and anyone wearing a zoot suit, eventually becoming an assault on the Mexican American community itself. Fights, with sometimes as many as fifty suiters, sailors, and marines broke out. There were deaths. Arrests were made. The fighting finally subsided in late June. For a time Los Angeles was off limits to all military personnel, and anyone caught wearing a zoot suit was given thirty-days' jail time.

As the boys were preparing to leave they were warned by Sergeant Bradley that if they even thought about getting into a fight they would spend the rest of their natural lives in the crossbar hotel. They caught a ride into Oceanside, then the bus to Los Angeles. After a short walk from the bus station to the movie district they had to make a decision as to which movie, *The Ox-Bow Incident* with Henry Fonda, or *They Got Me Covered* with Bob Hope. Davis wanted to see *The Ox-Bow Incident*. Thad and Rat wanted to see the Bob Hope movie. Thad told Davis that he had read *The Ox-Bow Incident* and would tell him all about it.

When they were coming out of the movie, it was dark. "What do we do now?"

Rat said, "Let's find the Paladium, listen to some music."

Thad said, "Okay with me."

Davis said, "Why not?"

They caught a cab and told the driver, "The Paladium, please," just like they knew what they were doing. Rat was the only one who had ever been in a cab. Before they got there, Rat had the cabbie stop at a liquor store. They gave him some money and had him buy them a pint of Old Crow. They got out in front of the Paladium and paid the cab fare. The marquee said Tommy Dorsey and His Orchestra, and since they were servicemen, the cover charge was waived, and they were escorted to a table near the dance floor. They ordered three cokes which were immediately spiked with liberal quantities of Old Crow.

Tommy Dorsey. Thad would have preferred Bob Wills and His Texas Playboys, but evidently Bob wasn't in town; he was probably still in Texas. After they had a few hits of the Old Crow the band played "Boogie Woogie Bugle Boy," dedicated to the service men present. Nice touch, Tommy. Then they played a soulful rendition of "You'd Be So Nice to Come Home To," which made Thad think of Lou Ann. Another fast number, Rat jumped up and said, "I gotta dance." He grabbed a woman sitting at the next table.

Thad told Davis, "He didn't even ask her, just pulled her out on the dance floor, for Christ's sake."

Turns out that Rat was one jitterbugging fool. Fortunately for the poor woman, she did an admirable job of keeping up. People stopped dancing and stood watching this marine and his partner, clapping in time with the music. When the music stopped, they applauded, Rat returned his out-of-breath dancing partner to her table, sat down, perspiring, and said, "I need a drink."

They played some slower dance music, and Rat's dancing partner asked him to dance. They danced once, twice. Rat came back to the table and announced that he was in love. It was then that Miss Dancing Partner's date showed up and nipped the romance in the bud. Rat was disappointed, but a couple more bourbon and cokes, and he seemed to get over it.

Having killed the pint of Old Crow, they stood outside the Paladium. "What do we do now?"

Rat said, "Find us a liquor store and buy another bottle."

Davis, the only sober one in the group, the one least drunk, anyhow, said, "C'mon, Rat, let's get something to eat. I'm starving."

"We can eat later. Let's find us a cab."

Fortunately, Thad and Rat eventually agreed with Davis. They had a nice dinner at an upscale restaurant and headed back to Camp Pendleton, back to the grinder.

The remaining weeks were more of the same. Week five was spent at the rifle range down the road at Camp Mathews. Even though the marines had qualified with the M-1 during boot camp, they were going to re-qualify. And Thad, having never qualified, looked forward to it. He had spent hours plunking cans, shooting at jack rabbits with his old hand-me-down .22 back in McCamey. At San Diego he and the other corpsmen trainees spent a day firing the —1. They learned how to break it down and clean it, no more than a familiarization exercise.

They shot at one hundred yards, two hundred yards, three hundred yards, and finally five hundred yards, standing, sitting, kneeling and prone. Thad had the basics down, but needed help adjusting his windage and elevation for the various distances. Since he was a sailor and didn't know diddly squat, according to the gunny, the gunny sat with him and helped him through adjusting his sights.

Once he had that down, he set out to prove to the gunny that he did know diddly squat and would qualify as an expert.

After the first day Thad began to have his doubts. He was okay with the prone and the sitting. But offhand and kneeling would need some work. He finally was comfortable with kneeling, which left the offhand (standing). Since they fired offhand from one hundred yards only, he figured that he could handle the rest enough to get him his expert's badge, and he was right. At the end of the week he did qualify as an expert, with only two others in the platoon scoring higher. The gunny said something about a blind hog finding an acorn.

Meanwhile poor Willis was having his problems. In the offhand position, he would anticipate the kick of the weapon and lunge into it, thereby screwing up his aim. While he insisted that he wasn't lunging, Sergeant Bradley got on his case. He told Willis to give him his weapon. "Turn around, and don't look. Willis, I'm going to put a live round in your rifle, or I may not." He slid the receiver back, let it slam home, and told Willis, "Okay, let's see you squeeze off a round."

Willis took his position, got his arm adjusted in his sling, took a breath, let out half of I. (*Looking good, Willis*), squeezed the trigger. *Click.* He jumped right off the firing line. "Don't lunge, huh, Willis?" Sergeant Bradley took off Willis' cover and smacked him repeatedly on the head with it.

At the week's end everyone had qualified, even Willis, and it was back to Camp Pendleton, packing their sea bags and boarding trucks bound for San Diego. There they practiced amphibious landings, got their shots, and were deemed ready to fight. They would be boarding ships in the days to follow, sailing off to who knew where. Finally Thad felt like he had been accepted—no longer half sailor, half marine, no longer Alexander the swoose. He was a marine, like it or not. He was their doc.

4
New Zealand

That September they boarded their troop transport and set sail. Captain Bartholomew told them that they were going to New Zealand for more training. *Is it possible to over-train?*

The two-week voyage was interesting and for some, even exiting, for the first three days. After that it was boring. There were weapons inspections, calisthenics, lectures, standing in the chow line, reading, lots of sleep, and Thad's getting to know more about the guys in the platoon.

Rat, it turns out, had been a member of a street gang, "The Blind Ducks." Hell's Kitchen boys, ages thirteen to nineteen. Skirmishes with other teen age gangs, petty burglaries, and rolling a drunk or two. Nothing serious. When Thad told Rat that "Blind Ducks" was the dumbest name for a gang that he'd ever heard, Rat agreed. He didn't pick the name. When asked about his name, Rat said his full name was Rudolf Alfons Trommler.

"You're right. Rat's good."

Thad asked him why he joined the Corps. Rat adjusted his steel-rimmed glasses and told him that one night, they decided to rob an eighteen-wheeled truck and trailer. They didn't know what it was carrying, but it must be valuable or the door wouldn't have a padlock on it. The truck was parked on a side street. It was two o'clock in the morning, not a soul in sight. They got after the lock with a pair of bolt cutters, making good progress, when the driver, who had been asleep inside the cab unbeknownst to the Blind Ducks, jumped out, waving a pistol, shouting. He cranked off a few rounds. Either he was a bad shot, the boys weren't more than fifty feet away, or he was just trying to put the fear of God in them. Either way it was effective. The boys scattered.

It was then that Rat decided if he was going to get shot at he might as well join the Marines where he could at least shoot back.

There was Roy Boy. Roy Boy had been raised on a farm in Georgia. He was a tall, thin country boy. Back at Pendleton, following their forced march up Nellies Tit and marching for three more hours without water, Roy Boy said, "I guess they're going to keep whipping us like chained-up hounds," and Thad knew immediately this was his kind of guy.

Thad asked what they raised on their farm.

"About a hundred acres of peanuts, a bunch of pecan trees, the rest of the two hundred acres is corn and beans."

"Lot of work?"

"You better believe it. Startin' in May, me and my four brothers and two sisters picked peanuts till our fingers was bleedin'. Then in the summer it was the sweet corn and field peas. Then come winter, we gathered pecans. Soon as I turned eighteen, I knew there had to be something better than picking peanuts. Hell, getting shot at is better than picking peanuts. I wanted to join the Navy, but a Marine recruiter stopped me and told me the Navy wouldn't have me because my parents were married. So I joined the Crotch."

"What'd your parents say?"

"Hell, Daddy said that if he wasn't so damn old, he'd go with me."

During the time aboard ship he got close to Jean Paul Boudreau, a coon ass from Lafayette Louisiana. Talked about pirogues, bayous, and eating crawdads. He sang some stupid song called "Jole Blon," which he said was the cajun national anthem, but his favorite was "Allons a Lafayette," which according to Boudreau, meant, "Let's go to Lafayette." *Whatever, Boudreau.* He had started grammar school not speaking a word of English and eventually attended LSU for a year. He spoke with a French accent, but his English was almost as good as Thad's. Maybe better.

They docked in Wellington, New Zealand, in late September, 1943, boarded trucks, and were transported to their camp outside of the city. In five-man tents they got their gear squared away. They were marched to chow, then to another lecture. Captain Bartholomew was telling them that soon they would be going into battle. "The first time for most of you, and some of you won't be coming back." he talked a little bit about Guadalcanal and the tradition of the Corps. "You've been well trained; I'm sure that you will serve with honor. The Japanese are tough, but you're tougher. They want to die for their Emperor. You don't want to die." *Advantage, Marines.* "I don't know where we're going. Probably won't know till we're underway. It's anticipated that we will be shipping out around the first of November, but that's not etched in stone. It may be sooner. Maybe later. Meanwhile, we'll continue with our training. You'll be given liberty in Wellington. I expect you to be on your best behavior, stay out of trouble. New Zealanders are a tolerant people. They appreciate what we are doing. Treat them with respect, and they will likewise treat you with respect. That's all I have for now. Questions?"

The following weeks were spent practicing amphibious landings, long marches through the New Zealand hills (nothing like Pendleton), spending time on the rifle range firing the M-1, the M-1 carbine and the BAR (Browning Automatic Rifle) and finally on the pistol range. Thad fired the 1911 Colt .45 semi-automatic for the first time. At fifteen yards, pretty good; thirty yards, okay; fifty yards, forget about it. Just hope the guy you're shooting at doesn't have a rifle. After firing several magazines and learning how to break the weapon down (no easy task) and clean it he was issued his own .45. He would go into battle armed with the .45 and two medical pouches.

After the second week Thad and Davis went on liberty into Wellington for the first time. Davis was six feet four and had movie-star good looks. Thad figured this guy had to be a magnet for pretty New Zealand girls. Thad had just turned twenty-one and Davis was twenty-two, the oldest among the platoon. Buying booze would not be a problem. Female companionship would be a snap, as the war had depleted the country of its young men. Thousands were already overseas and more were leaving in regular shipments. Girls were left without boyfriends, wives without husbands.

Their first stop was the bar at the St. George Hotel. First a nip of scotch, which was rationed, followed by a few warm beers. Then it was time to seek female companionship. They caught a cab and asked the driver where they might find same. "How about a nightclub?"

"A nightclub will do just fine."

The driver dropped them at the Majestic Cabaret. There was a swing band, not bad. *Have to tell Rat about this place.* The place was full of women. Thad asked the nearest pretty girl to dance while Davis opted to sit it out. Turned out that Davis was a lousy dancer and was painfully shy, to boot.

After a few dances, Thad explained to Dolores, his dancing partner, that his friend was bashful and did she have a friend that might be willing to take a chance with this tall, shy, good-looking marine. She said she had just the girl. They returned to the table, and Davis was introduced to Margaret. He stood, shook hands with Margaret, and Thad expected him to shuffle a foot and say, "Aw, shucks." Thad and Dolores danced. They sipped their drinks. Davis and Margaret talked.

After an hour or so, it was decided that it was time for something to eat. They left the Majestic, found a nice restaurant, ate their steaks, talked some more, and what do you know? Margaret was a shy as Davis. A relationship made in heaven.

In the weeks to follow, Thad and Dolores visited the bistros, speakeasies, and nightclubs while Davis and Margaret opted for sightseeing trips, cab rides through the countryside. Thad wasn't falling in love, not by a long shot, but the companionship was what he and every other marine longed for. He had his doubts about Davis, however. Though he never talked about it, Thad thought that he might have fallen for this shy, New Zealand girl.

Finally their orders came. They were to board ship on first day of November.

A final liberty to Wellington. Thad and Davis said their goodbyes to Dolores and Margaret, everyone promising to write. Back to camp they packed their seabags, cleaned their weapons, and the next morning they boarded the troop transport, saluted the colors, the office of the deck, and found their sleeping quarters. Back on deck, the crowd on the dock waved, a band played the Marine Hymn, and that was it. The ship slowly pulled away, New Zealand finally became a spec on the horizon.

Wherever they were headed, The marines would be led ashore by Colonel David Monroe Shoup. A squat, red-faced man with a bull neck, a hard-boiled, profane shouter of orders, he would carry the biggest burden. On his judgment and ability would depend the lives of several thousand men, and ultimately whether the battle was won or lost. Colonel Shoup would be awarded the Medal of Honor for his heroic actions on Tarawa and would later become the Commandant of the Marine Corps.

On 19 November they were shown a topographic model of an island, smaller than New York's Central Park. Captain Bartholomew told them that the island's name was Betio, and this was where they were headed. Sort of looked like a skinny pork chop with an airfield down the middle. Some said it looked like a bird. The beaches were all identified—Red 1, Red 2, Red 3, Green Beach, Black 1, and Black 2. The captain told them that they would be landing at Red Beach No. 3. "Navy ships will be shelling the place. Navy planes will be bombing it, hopefully destroying all opposition, but it ain't going to happen. They've had years to fortify the place. The landing craft will deposit you on the beach. You'll continue inland, secure the airstrip, then the remainder of the island. Questions?"

"How long should this take us?"

"Maybe a few hours, a few days, maybe a week. Maybe a month. Depends on how many Japs are on the island and how well they're dug in. Remember, they're going to fight to the death. They don't believe in surrender. There's going to be a lot of losses on both sides."

There were no more questions.

Then came the Second Marine Division's Commander, General Julian Smith. His message: "The division has been selected because of its excellence, both in training and on the battlefield. Their confidence in us will not be betrayed. You are well trained and fit for the tasked assigned you. You will quickly overrun the Japanese forces. You will decisively defeat and destroy the treacherous enemies of our country. Your success will add new laurels to the traditions of our beloved Corps. Good luck, and God bless you all."

On the morning of 20 November they heard "Up and at 'em" at 0400. Then there was breakfast of steak and eggs, they got their gear squared away, went up on deck where they had one more weapons inspection. Thad checked his two medical pouches for the last time—battle dressings, sulfa powder, cloth tourniquets, and morphine. He could have carried a carbine, but opted for the .45. He watched the hellish bombardment and awaited his turn to climb down into the landing craft. Finally came the call, "Away all boats. Land the landing force."

Bloody Tarawa

Tarawa is located approximately 2,500 miles southwest of Hawaii. It isn't an island, but a series of barren islets, part of the Gilbert Islands. The largest of the islets is Betio (which rhymes with ratio) measuring less than 3 miles in length and ½ mile in width, about four hundred acres, roughly the size of Central Park.

The invasion of Tarawa (Betio) in November, 1943 by the Second Marine Division, commanded by Major General Julian C. Smith, was the first amphibious assault in the Pacific in which the Marines faced opposition from the beach. The troops would be led ashore by Colonel David Monroe Shoup.

Shoup and Colonel Merritt A. Edson, Julian Smith's Chief of Staff, proposed a landing plan that featured a sustained preliminary bombardment of several day's duration. General Smith took this proposal to the planning conference held in Pearl Harbor in early October for the principal officers involved in Operation Galvanic, the code name for the assault on Betio. The Marines were stunned to hear the restrictions imposed on their assault by CinCPac (Commander in Chief, U.S. Pacific Command, Admiral Chester W. Nimitz). Nimitz declared that the requirement for strategic surprise limited preliminary bombardment of Betio to about three hours on the morning of D-Day. It was also decided by General Holland "Howlin' Mad" Smith, senior to Julian Smith, to hold the Sixth Marines as corps reserves.

All of Julian Smith's tactical options had been stripped away. The Second Marine Division was compelled to make a frontal assault into the teeth of Betio's defenses with an abbreviated, preparatory bombardment and less than a 2-to-1 one superiority in troops. Julian Smith shared the agonies of the Pearl Harbor with his wife. As she recalled:

> Julian told me several times that he hoped history would bring out the truth regarding the tactical plans for Tarawa. His battle plans had been discarded, and he received verbal orders to engage in a full frontal assault, even though there were some who had doubts that the island could be taken under these conditions, for it violated all good doctrine. That is precisely why Julian asked Holland Smith to put his orders in writing, for if the assault proved unsuccessful he didn't want to end up the scapegoat and become known as the general most responsible for the slaughter of his own troops.

Many lessons were learned from Tarawa. First, naval gunfire, as powerful as it was, was often too short and often ineffective against the man-made and natural defenses of the Japanese-held islands. Secondly, Major General Holland "Howlin' Mad" Smith argued for the use of amtracs rather than Higgins Boats, as transportation from ship to shore was realized as the most efficient mode to get the marines to the beach and also to handle the difficult tides and treacherous reefs. Also the concept of "More is better than less" was demonstrated at Tarawa, as many of the amtracs were disabled before they could land their troops. Naval and Marine planners overestimated the effects of naval gunfire and aerial bombardment and underestimated the Japanese will to fight to the last man.

Military necessity dictated that the Tarawa atoll would become a focal point in the Pacific war. The Japanese had built an airfield on Betio Island. The crude strip was unremarkable, but whoever controlled that facility could influence the sea-lanes to the South Pacific.

There were risks. This landing would entail the first major American assault against a coral atoll. The tactical implications would severely test the nation's new amphibious doctrine, and for the first thirty-six hours the amphibious assault of Tarawa hung in precarious balance. The Japanese garrison, fighting to almost the last man, sold their lives dearly, making the marines pay for every square yard of sand and coral.

The Japanese were typically commanded by a Navy captain or commander, as the Imperial Japanese Navy provided land units in the Pacific war. These naval land units had the best training of all Japanese forces, and these men destined to defend Tarawa seemed exceptionally proficient. They were Imperial Japanese Marines, the best Tojo had. They were ably led, thoroughly trained, admirably proficient with their entire range of weaponry, skilled in camouflage and concealment, and possessed a fierce fighting spirit. That they failed to recognize the identical combat qualities in the ranks of the amphibious force rumbling toward them was their one great mistake. Otherwise, these sailors were spoiling for a fight.

The Japanese had recognized Tarawa's strategic importance as a perimeter outpost as early as thirteen months before the American invasion. To the extent possible, the Japanese military leaders accorded Tarawa top priority and supplied the forces on Betio with generous amounts of troops, weapons, fortification materials, engineering expertise, and labor. The Marines would not encounter a more sophisticated series of defensive positions on any subsequent island until they reached Iwo Jima some two years later. Yard for yard, Betio was the toughest fortified position the Marines would ever face.

In addition to concrete fortification structures, the Japanese also used natural materials like coral rock and coconut logs. They left Betio's trees alone, and a boat section was sent to the outer islands daily to retrieve five thousand coconut logs. These became the principal element of a seawall built almost completely around the island's perimeter. They also used the logs to build many of their firing positions.

The Japanese planned to defend Betio at the water's edge. "Knock out the landing boats with mountain gunfire, tank guns, and infantry guns, then concentrate all fires on the enemy's landing point, and destroy him at the water's edge."

Admiral Keiji Shibasaki commanded the forces defending Betio. He had all the engineering experience than he would ever need, but more than that, he was simply a warrior. He was exceptionally good in improving defensive coordination and lifting troop spirits. He worked the troops hard, dividing the day into construction projects and military training, principally marksmanship and gunnery. The garrison remarkably increased its fighting capability, and they were full of confidence.

Admiral Shibasaki boasted, "One million Americans couldn't take Tarawa in a hundred years."

A handful of marines took the island in seventy-six hours.

Marines of the Second Division landed on Tarawa on 20

November 1943. By the time the marines landed, the Japanese had 4800 Navy troops on the island, including 2,600 men of the Special Naval Landing Force—Japanese marines. They had constructed beach defenses of concrete and barbed wire fences to stop the amphibious craft. A formidable array of heavy caliber harbor defense guns were in place. As the landing crafts approached, Japanese officers leaped up on top of the seawall brandishing swords, challenging the marines to meet them hand-to-hand. The Americans were storming directly into a hornets' nest.

Heavy naval bombardment and carrier-based fighter/bomber strikes preceded the invasion. Six million pounds of explosives were hurled at the island from naval gunfire. Because of heavy dust and smoke Navy pilots couldn't see their targets. Thus they spent very little time over Tarawa. The bombardment was effective enough to keep the enemy's head down and allow some of the first three waves of marines to land on the beaches. However, the Japs were still able to destroy many of the amtracs that were launched during the first three waves. Because of the low tide and depth of the water at the coral reef, Higgins Boats could make it no further. The marines had to either wade to shore, or, if they were lucky, transfer to one of the amtracs. Because of low tide, the marines waded ashore in a hail of gunfire, suffering heavy casualties. It was here that the phrase, "Bloody Tarawa," was born. As marines landed on the beach, some were cut down by murderous defensive fire. Others were cut off from their units, and because of bad communications marines were unable to move to their proper beaches.

The Japanese Commander, Admiral Shibasaki, was said to have been killed on the first day by U.S. Navy planes. The Japanese suffered communication problems as well on D-Day. Because of the loss of Admiral Shibasaki and poor communications, these two factors may have prevented the Japs from their only chance to defend Tarawa. Many believe that if the Japs had carried out a counterattack that first night it might have succeeded . Several Japanese were able set up machine guns on the seven-hundred-foot-long pier. Marine troops were getting hit from the rear as well. It wasn't until midnight of D-Day-plus-1 that the rising tide enabled Higgins boats to bring badly needed supplies and reserve troops to support the marines on the beach.

The division would suffer a thousand casualties a day at Betio, the highest casualty rate sustained by any division in the war. After the battle, interrogators asked one captured Japanese when he thought the tide of battle had turned in favor of the invaders. "When the dying Americans kept coming, one after the another," was the alleged reply. The best weapon the marines brought to Tarawa proved to be their inherent aggressiveness, ingrained from boot camp, enhanced by their combat leaders. In this respect, the Joint Chiefs and America got exactly what they sought, "battle-tested shock troops."

After three days of bloody battle and heavy U.S. casualties enough marines were able to make it ashore and sweep the atoll, aided by tanks and howitzers. By the afternoon of 23 November, Tarawa was fully in American hands and the Second Marine Division had been decimated.

CORPSMAN!

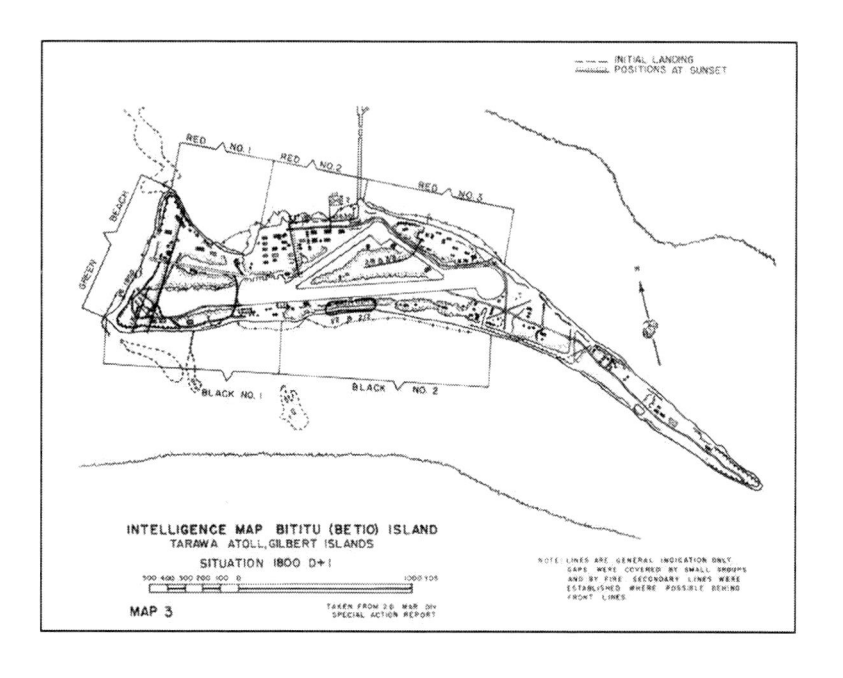

5
20 November 1943

From aboard ship, miles off shore, they watched the island blow up, like fans viewing a spectacle. Battleships, destroyers, every ship imaginable. They were throwing everything they had at the tiny speck of land. "Get some, Navy! Hell, they may sink the whole damn island, and we'll all go home."

Many senior naval officers were optimistic about the outcome. "We do not intend to neutralize the island; we do not intend to destroy it;" boasted one admiral, "Gentlemen, we will obliterate it."

But General Smith had heard enough of these boasts. He stood and addressed the meeting. "Even though you naval officers do come to about one thousand yards, I remind you that you have a little armor. I want you to know that the marines are crossing the beach with bayonets, and the only armor they'll have is a khaki shirt!"

All of a sudden the big guns stopped, and here came the planes, not just a few planes, maybe a hundred planes. SBD Dauntless' Helldivers dropped their big bombs on an island that must have been dead a half hour ago. The dive bombers lined up thousands of feet above Betio, pointed their noses down, and dived singly, in pairs or in threes. Near the end of their dives they released their bombs and pulled up gracefully, then headed back to the carriers for more bombs. Then came the new Grumman Hellcats making their runs, their machine guns spitting hundreds of fifty-caliber bullets a minute. Surely, nothing could live through such destructive power.

The story of the battle of Tarawa will forever be linked to the tides that remained so unpredictably low for the first forty-eight hours of the amphibious assault. Julian Smith, given no alternative to the landing date of 20 November, hoped that morning for a rising tide high enough to provide unobstructed passage of boats as well as amphibious tractors. It was not to be. In essence while the first three waves of assault troops in amtracs crossed the reef without incident, the marines never got the necessary four feet of water over the reef to permit passage of the Higgins boats transporting the balance of the assault forces, supporting arms, and reinforcements.

What they got, instead, was a tide that never rose a foot above mean level. It has been called "The Tide That Failed." As a fatal consequence no landing boats could cross the reef. Thousands of marines had to wade the six-to-eight hundred yards to shore, and hundreds fell to Japanese gunners.

From the LSTs (Landing Ship, Tank), forty-two amtracs (LVTs, Landing Vehicle, Tracked), carrying eighteen marines each, were launched and constituted the first wave. One hundred yards behind them came the second wave of twenty-four amtracs. Then another one hundred yards, the third wave of twenty-one amtracs. The thirty-six-foot-long wooden Higgins boats comprised the fourth-tenth waves. If the operation went according to plan, three thousand marines would be ashore in thirty minutes, followed by another six thousand by noon. According to plan.

At 8:24 the first wave of amtracs crossed the line of departure and churned toward Betio, still six thousand yards away. Even though they had received fire, the amtracs and Higgins boats sustained little damage, leading the marines to cling to their hopes for a quick operation. They faced an open stretch of water to the reef, the reef itself, and a final run-in of seven hundred yards to what, hopefully, would be a quiet beach.

The Japanese silently watched their enemy draw nearer to the reef. Fortunately for the Japanese, the waters at the reef had receded, exposing the hard, sharp coral. The unpredictable tides had worked in their favor. They waited for the American landing boats to grind to a sudden stop on Betio's protective reef. The Americans would be sitting ducks for the Japanese guns that would tear into them while still seven hundred yards from shore. The enemy would suffer dearly.

The elaborate defenses prepared by the Japanese were impressive. Mine fields and long strings of barbed wire protected beach approaches. Tank traps protected heavily command bunkers and firing positions inland from the beach. Everywhere there were pillboxes, nearly five hundred of them, most fully covered by logs, steel plates, and sand.

At 8:55, fifteen minutes before the first American touched Betio's sands, the naval bombardment was halted. It was feared that the excessive amount of smoke would blind naval gunners and that shells would fall into the marines headed to shore.

When the shelling ceased, the Japanese took advantage of the opportunity to position themselves carefully. They placed their machine gunners and riflemen in the most advantageous spots. They would horribly punish the Americans, without gunfire shielding them.

To say that the Japanese were shocked while witnessing the next development, would be an understatement. Instead of stalling at the reef, the American landing craft rammed into it, churned up and over, and continued toward the island. They had never seen landing craft with that capability, but here was the enemy brushing aside the reef as if it wasn't even there.

The enemy defenders, recovering from their shock, opened up on the approaching, slow moving, LVT's as they crossed the reef with seemingly every available gun on the island: eight-inch naval rifles, anti-boat guns, artillery and howitzers, 13 mm heavy machine guns, 7.7 mm light machine guns and knee mortars. They systematically and methodically began blowing the little landing crafts out of the water. They were, indeed, horribly punishing the Americans.

It took an hour and a half for Thad's Higgins boat to reach its rendezvous point off the beach where it joined other assault boats for the landing. For Thad and thirty-five others, that was plenty of time to get sick and vomit on each other.

Suddenly, the Higgins boat idled to a stop, and the boat driver announced that he couldn't go any further because the water was too shallow.

"You gotta be shittin' me. Must be a thousand yards to the beach."

"You can transfer to an amtrac for the rest of the trip."

During their short wait, they watched the disaster unfolding before them. Flames rose from body-draped amtracs that blazed out of control. Marines crawled out of burning tractors with their clothing on fire. Amtracs ran into each other. Some Navy coxswains, seeing the slaughter just ahead, stopped their boats outside the reef and ordered the troops off. The marines, many loaded with radios or mortars or extra ammunition, sank immediately in deep water. Most drowned. The Japs destroyed or disabled most of the eighty-seven amtracs during the first three waves.

Finally, an amtrac pulled up alongside. Thad and seventeen others climbed into the little, tracked vehicle. The rest of them would have to wait for another amtrac to pick them up or start wading.

After what seemed to be a very short ride, the amtrac boss said, "See that old hulk of that Jap freighter? I'll let you out there and pick up some more men. You guys can wade in from there."

"You can't put us out here!"

"Yes, I can. Get out."

They scurried over the side of the amtrac into water that was neck deep, and started wading. Several Japanese were able to make it out to the grounded Jap freighter and set up machine guns. The marines were getting hit from the front and the rear. No sooner had they hit the water than the Jap machine guns opened up on them. While bullets peppered the water around them, it was slow wading in such deep water, sometimes pushing dead bodies aside, holding weapons over their heads, and Thad keeping his medical pouches dry the best he could. Soon they would be larger targets as they reached shallow water. He was scared like he had never been scared before. They were also receiving fire from the seven-hundred-yard pier to their right. Thad saw a handful marines leap onto the seaplane ramp that extended from the piers' end. They tossed grenades into the enemy positions and steadily moved down the pier toward shore, ducking behind gasoline drums or crates as they scampered along. They knocked out machine-gun nests and returned back to the reef, but more Japanese occupied the structure after they left.

As men left their amtracs, they stepped directly into the paths of several Japanese machine guns. They were raked from all directions. People were getting killed wholesale. Marines were floating in the water face down. The dead appeared to outnumber the living. So many bullets splattered the water near Thad that it reminded him of raindrops in a barrel, or shooting fish in a barrel.

The assault's commander, Colonel David Monroe Shoup, had trouble reaching land. At the reef he commandeered an amtrac returning with a load of wounded marines, but when he jumped into the craft, he saw that most of the marines were dead. He ordered the crew chief and gunner to help him toss the bodies overboard, then returned to the reef to transfer the wounded and pick up his staff.

As the amtrac headed toward shore, heavy Japanese fire damaged the craft. Shoup ordered everyone to jump into the lagoon and head toward the pier. He encouraged every marine near him and chastised those he felt like were holding back. "Are there any of you cowardly sons of bitches got the guts to follow a colonel of the marines?"

The final one hundred yards to the beach proved to be the most dangerous. A shell concussion knocked him to the water and wrenched his knee, but the gutsy colonel rejected help and splashed onto the beach around noon.

As he arrived, another close explosion hurled shrapnel into Shoup's legs and killed two men next to him. He again refused help from his staff, and moved a short way inland to set up his command post.

Shoup tried to evaluate what had occurred to this point in the battle. He obviously had suffered heavy casualties, especially among the officers. He faced a dwindling number of amtracs to ferry in reinforcements and ammunition, and the Higgins boats with men and supplies were held up at the reef. Would his men be able to repulse the expected counter attack, or would they be destroyed first?

The dynamic colonel alternately encouraged some men and chastised others, depending on their performance. One time he slapped a pair of legs protruding from a pile of rubble. He continued to slap the legs until finally a frightened young corporal peered out.

"I'm Colonel Shoup. What's your name?" When the man responded, he asked him where his mother lived, and added, "Well, do you think she'd be proud of you, curled up in a hole like that, no damn use to anybody?"

The corporal agreed she would not. When Shoup, chewing his ever-present unlit cigar, inquired about his squad, the marine informed him they were all dead.

"Well, why don't you get yourself another squad?"

The corporal said he didn't know how.

Shoup points to a group of marines hugging the seawall, not moving at all, and said, "Pick out a man, then another and another. Just say, 'Follow me.' When you've got a squad, report to me."

The corporal nodded and disappeared down the beach. Shoup returned to other matters, never expecting to see the young man again, but a short time later, the young man returned.

"I got me a squad, sir."

When Shoup asked where his new squad was, the corporal pointed to two shell craters not far away. Shoup handed him a mission and sent him on his way.

He had helped a young man overcome near-paralyzing fear, help him realize what he needed to do, and then under most dangerous conditions, the corporal carried out his duties. That, in his opinion, was how you won wars.

6

Thad finally reached the beach, and he marveled at still being alive. At the base of the seawall, he fell into a fetal position and tried to cover his head. Explosions. Machine-gun fire. He wanted the explosions and the machine gun fire to stop. He didn't want to be here.

"Move!" Someone shouted, "Move!"

He didn't want to move. He wanted to vomit. There were fallen marines lying on the beach. Behind him more marines were floating in the shallow water, which was beginning to take on a reddish tint. Amtracs and Higgins boats were being blown out of the water.

"Move!"

He began to crawl forward. Half blinded by the smoke, he got to his feet and started running, finally making it over the seawall. He tripped and fell over a body. Another body. *Jesus. The guy is still holding his M-1 and his face is gone.*

Corpsman!" Someone is shouting, "Corpsman!"

Running in a crouch, he was trying to find where the shout was coming from. He passed a marine lying on his back. He was not shouting. Finally he reached the wounded man. He was no longer shouting. He was holding both hands over his stomach, trying to tell him something, but Thad couldn't understand him. Was he crying? Too much noise, and now he felt the explosions rather than heard them. He tried to move the wounded man's hands, but he resisted. Finally, he removes his hands so that he can look at the wound. A hole. Not too large. A lot of blood. The corpsman rips open the marine's utility jacket and applies sulfa powder and a pressure bandage, and tried to get him to drink from his canteen. He took a small drink and tried to swallow. He gently rolled the man over on his side. There was a large hole in his pack, and the back of the dungaree jacket was soaked. The exit wound. Vital organs? The man tried to sit up. The corpsman held his canteen to the man's lips. He shook his head. The marine was still crying and trying to tell him something. He finally seemed to relax. He had stopped crying.

Thad still wanted to throw up. He couldn't. But he could cry.

He fell into the nearest bomb crater where he was joined by a marine. Then another. Then two more. The marines were cranking off rounds. There were explosions, machine-gun fire, the ka-ching of the clips being ejected from the M-1s. There was constant re-loading and firing, the automatic fire of a BAR. Thad didn't know if they were hitting anything or not. He was not about to look. Stay down. Stay safe. A boot fell into the hole. *Jesus Christ! There's still a foot in it. Get it out of here!* Thad grabbed it and tossed it out of the crater.

The four marines, after several minutes of firing, left the hole running, firing from the hip, until they reached another crater. Two of them fell into it while the other two continued on. Thad followed and jumped into the hole with the first two. Sand was being kicked up all around them from rifle fire, the sound of bullets slicing through the air along with the damn explosions. Thad figured that if the mortars and artillery didn't kill him, the little fuckers with rifles would.

He watched the two marines still running. One of them dropped, dropped like he had fallen out of a tree. "Shit! I can't leave him out there, and I sure as hell can't go out there now. Be like one of them little fucking bears at a shooting gallery. I don't even know if he's still alive."

The fallen marine lifted his head and seemed to look around, then lowered his head again.

The marine with the BAR said that he thought he knew where the firing was coming from and would give him covering fire while he went to recover the wounded man. *Swell. Must be twenty, twenty-five yards.* He left his pouches in the hole and took off. Running in a half crouch, he reached the wounded marine, grabbed him under the arms and began dragging him back to the crater. Rounds impacting in the sand all around him, finally he reached the hole and fell into it while the other two reached out and dragged the now-unconscious man into the crater.

While catching his breath, Thad felt a pulse in the man's neck, and then it simply stopped. He was no longer breathing. He had been struck in the mouth, the bullet entering the back of his throat. No teeth were broken, and there was a lot of blood. The guy looked as though he were lying there, looking up at the smoke and dust covering the sky. He was yet another marine that would be forever nineteen.

Everywhere Thad looked there was movement. Men running, shooting, screaming, falling. Smoke and dust hung in the air making it hard to breathe. More landing crafts were off loading their precious cargo. *Welcome to this stinking corner of hell. The more the merrier.* There were marines still unable to get off the beach, unable to penetrate inland. The congestion delayed the landings of the following waves and tied up the American assault at the reef. With nowhere to go, the marines were easy targets. At this point, the prognosis appeared bleak.

A Marine captain brazenly stood on top of the seawall, fully exposed to enemy fire, smoking his pipe and shouting for the men to follow. He swore and called some of the men cowards in an effort to prod them on, and tried to show with his example that enemy bullets were not to be feared. Men begged him to get off the damn wall, but he remained at his post, shouting, cussing and prodding. Here and there a few marines responded and slid up and over the logs, but many remained frozen. Japanese machine-gun bullets riddled the captain's throat and head.

Nearby a platoon of marines had set up their machine guns and were firing at the nearest Japanese pillboxes less than twenty yards away. They destroyed a handful of enemy positions, but the Japanese had too much firepower. In only a few moments the machine guns were silenced. Most of that platoon had been wiped out. None had advanced more than one hundred feet. One could trace the route taken by the machine gunners by following the trail of bodies. They died before the battle was thirty minutes old.

Thad had become separated from his company. He hollered, "Charlie Company!" over and over, hoping that someone would hear him over the clamor and holler back. Still in the crater with the three marines, one of them dead, he finally worked up the courage to raise his head and look over the edge, hoping to see someone, anyone he knew.

Another call. "Corpsman!" It seemed to be coming from his right, but he couldn't be sure. Then again. "Corpsman!" It was coming from his right.

He clambered out of the hole and ran in the direction of the shouting. He heard it again and jumped into the crater. Two marines. One of the marine's trouser legs were soaked with blood. Thad ripped them apart with his K-BAR. Long gashes, deep pulsing holes covered the marine's thighs. He began dressing the man's legs, and the man said, "Doc, I'm okay. Help Sockwell. Man, he's really fucked up."

Sockwell was seriously fucked up. He was dead. He had a shrapnel hole clear through his chest, up high and more shrapnel in his face and head. He checked Sockwell's buddy's wounds again and told him to hang loose, and they would get him out of there.

Thad saw a marine with a radio on his back running toward a fallen palm tree. Lots of palm trees. The ones left standing looked sick. There were half palm trees, no palm trees, just stumps, and all the rest were leaning awkwardly and looking sick. The marine with the radio was Boudreau. *What the hell's he doing with a radio?*

He caught up with him as the Cajun was shouting into the radio, "Canary, this is Canary three. How do you read? Over," all the while grinning at Thad.

Jesus, how can the man smile while the world is blowing up all around him?

He took the handset away from his ear and said, "*Bon jour*, Doc. *Comment allez-vous?*"

Thad shouted, "You're no radio operator. Where's Booth?"

"He bought it as soon as he hit the beach. I picked up his radio."

"Can you reach the company?"

"Patience. Patience, *mon cher*. I'm trying, and I hope I don't have to change frequencies. I must have slept through that part of radio procedure."

"Try harder." A radio operator with an accent. Perfect.

After several more "Canaries," Boudreau was finally having a conversation with someone. He said "Roger, out," and hooked the handset back on the radio and told Thad "That was Captain Bartholomew. He's further down the beach. That way, I believe. Shall we go and try to find him?"

"After you."

They took off running, landing crafts on their right, still coming in, belching out marines, others, having delivered their precious cargo, going back out to the awaiting ships. "To pick up more marines? Good." As they ran, Boudreau with his M-1, the radio on his back, and Thad holding on to his medical pouches, ducking, sometimes falling, dodging shell craters, they were looking for anyone they knew, hoping that they were close.

The company had all climbed down into the landing crafts, one squad after another. The little boats circled, waited for everyone to be loaded then headed toward the beach. The only way they could have been separated from the rest of the company is if the boat driver joined up with the wrong bunch of boats while circling. Surely not. Then again, in the chaos and bedlam that followed after leaving the amtracs, anything was possible. Thad was lucky to find Boudreau.

Keep running. A rolling stone gathers no moss. A running corpsman gathers no bullets. Winded, they fell into a crater. *No shortage of craters, ready-made foxholes.* Before they had caught their breath, someone close by hollered, "Boudreau! Get you ass over here with that radio." It was Gunny Mancillas, not more than a few yards away. An uprooted palm tree was lying across the gunny's crater, making for protection, at least from rifle fire. A well-placed mortar round, however, would be a different story.

They jumped into the crater with Gunny, and he asked Boudreau, shouting to be heard above the constant explosions, "What the fuck are you doing with the radio?" and asked him if he could raise the captain. PFC Boudreau, ever the happy coon ass, said, "*Bien sur*," raised "Canary" on the radio, and gave Gunny the hand set.

Gunny repeatedly said, "Yes, sir," and "No, sir," and finally gave the handset back to Boudreau. "Captain said we got to get the rest of the platoon rounded up and try to join the rest of the company further down the beach." He asked Thad if he'd had to treat any men from the platoon.

He said no, but Boudreau told him that Booth was dead.

The company runner, Mouse, "Shit House Mouse," the smallest man in the company, between explosions, fell into the crater and told them the company was going to try to form up about fifty yards further down the beach. He was gone again, shouting the same message to everyone he could find, whether they were in Charlie Company or not.

Gunny looked at Thad and Boudreau and said, "You ready?"

They both gave him a nod, whether they were ready or not, climbed out, and there they went. The gunny, running without the burden of a radio or medical pouches, holding his M-1 like it was a baton ready to pass it off to the next runner, finally jumped into a crater. He turned to see Thad and Boudreau zigging and zagging, attempting to dodge bullets. Out of breath, not to mention scared out of their minds, they made it to the crater and jumped in. The captain's voice came over the radio, telling Boudreau that he had them in sight and to sit tight. They had found the company. Now what?

Eventually, Lt. Stanley found them and told them to form up in squads the best they could and wait for the word. The lieutenant was a graduate of some ivy league college, a part-time prima-donna and a full-time prick. He had busted Rat down from PFC to private for failing to salute. *See how he holds up after we get the "word."*

Perhaps the word would be to storm across the island, capture the airfield, kill all the Japs, and go home. Or to sit tight, as the captain had suggested, and wait. Wait for the word.

The word came. They moved out and made good progress, surprising several groups of Japanese who scrambled out of their temporary shelters in trenches and wrecked buildings. They continued, crossed the taxiway, and took up defensive positions behind log revetments parallel to the main runway. The revetments and bomb craters made for good protection, "good" being relative.

Navy aircraft, under orders not to damage the precious runway, still screaming overhead, mistook the small cluster of marines hiding in the revetments for Japanese, and would bomb them on the way in and strafe them on the way out until they were called off. Then the Japanese opened up with accurate rifle fire. A well-aimed round struck Hernandez' M-1 below the rear sight and broke it in half. Hernandez said, "It felt like I had stuck my fingers in an electric socket."

"Here comes one of our tanks!" yelled one of the marines manning the revetment. But it was a Japanese tank. It had come around the end of the revetment from out of nowhere. A rifle grenade was fired at it and missed. By then, the tank had moved right into the middle of this collection of marines, and a BAR man jumped up on top of the moving tank and tried to stuff a grenade through the hatch. He was blown off by a burst of machine gun fire, and the tank kept moving. It rolled into a crater, unoccupied by now, and stalled. Marines surrounded the tank, when suddenly the engine caught, and it clanked away, toward the beach.

A small group of Japanese behind the seawall had been sniping at the marines. Now their leader obviously figured it was time for one of their banzai things. Destroy these foreign devils. He shouted, "Follow me!" or the equivalent, and leaped over the barricade, waving his sword. His men didn't follow, and he found himself alone on the beach. For some reason the marines didn't fire at him. Disbelief? He swung his sword at the astonished marines, and quickly jumped back over the seawall before they could come to their senses, and surely commenced with a serious Japanese ass-chewing.

While attempting to scale the four-foot sea wall, Charlie Company's third platoon was caught in a cross fire, decimating entire squads. Thad watched as a marine with two packs of dynamite charged a Jap machine-gun position that had been firing at the marines still in the water. He lobbed one charge and then the other directly into the emplacement, eliminating the Japanese. The marine sustained a wound in his left arm and shrapnel wounds to his face. There was still a more dangerous gun emplacement further inland firing steadily at the wading marines. This same marine, with two more dynamite charges in hand, crawled forward and managed to stuff one of the charges through the firing slits, destroying the gun and crew, but he took another bullet through the same arm, and the fourth charge blew up in his hand just as he threw it.

With those guns being silenced, Thad began treating the survivors, some with superficial flesh wounds, some with wounds that would soon become fatal. Rat had come with him to give him covering fire. He used pressure bandages, sulfa, tourniquets, comforting words. Rat called out to him, "Patterson's hurt bad, man." When Thad reached Rat and Patterson, Rat was holding Patterson's head in his lap, ignoring the sporadic gun fire, telling Thad he had to do something. Patterson was a New York boy, just like Rat. Thad squatted over the man who was unconscious but breathing, a bullet wound in his upper chest. He applied the sulfa powder and a pressure bandage, all the while Rat insisting that the marine was coming out of it and to give him a shot of morphine.

"Nothing I can do except call him an emergency and try to get him out of here. Can't shoot him up with morphine, not when he's already out. Might kill him. We've done all we can do here, Rat. We'll find stretcher bearers for him and get back to the company." (Members of the Second Marine Division's band served as stretcher bearers. It was dangerous work. Twelve of these band members became casualties themselves.)

Reluctantly Rat got up, told Patterson, who couldn't hear his friend, that he was going to be okay. "You've got one of them wounds that will get you out of here and back to stateside."

No sooner had they made it back to what was left of Charlie company hunkered down behind the log revetments, than they were ordered to move out. Up and over any obstacles that lay between them and their goal, the goal being to kill every Jap on this tiny little island and get off of it. A battle had to be won, and the only way to do it was to rush forward, taking land from those who didn't want to give it up. The sand was littered with thousands of palm fronds, among the twisted and shredded palm trees, along with pieces of metal. Fires raged everywhere. and a thick blanket of dark smoke hung over the entire island, making it hard to breathe.

It seemed that the battle raged on every square foot, most often against unseen opponents. Snipers hid in hundreds of spider holes scattered about the island and strapped themselves in palm trees. On Betio, there was no such thing as a safe place behind the lines. The back lines were, for all intents and purposes, the front lines. Japanese and Americans fought mere yards from each other.

The marines started the nasty, deadly job of knocking out the hundreds of Japanese pillboxes on the island, knowing that sooner or later, the Japanese would simply lack the strength to stop the marines from moving forward, no matter the cost. Thad saw Sergeant Bradley run across an open area toward a machine-gun nest that had been firing at them.

With the machine gun still firing, Thad was thinking, *You ain't invisible, Sarge.*

Bradley made it to the machine gun, jammed a grenade

through the firing slit and dove over the top. The grenade exploded. The firing stopped.

If he ain't invisible, maybe he's Superman.

Moments after killing a Jap with a hand grenade, Roy Boy felt a bullet pass through one side of his jacket and out the other. Figuring a sniper had him in his sights, he collapsed and lay as if he were dead for several minutes, then jumped up and ran for a nearby hole as bullets nipped at his heels. When he checked to see if he was wounded, Roy Boy noticed that the letters on his uniform, USMC, had been ripped apart by the bullet.

Thad watched a group of nearby marines that seemed to be screwing together six foot joints of pipe, and shoving it out of their foxhole toward a Jap pillbox. "What the hell is that? What are they doing?"

Gunny told him, "That, my friend, is a bangalore torpedo. Watch this."

They kept adding joints of pipe and kept shoving until it was through the opening of the pillbox. Thad could see the Jap machine gunner wrestling with the business end of the pipe, trying to shove it back out, when the damn thing exploded in his hands, killing him and his two companions.

"Ain't that something!"

As the day wore on, marine losses were becoming unacceptable if not critical. A mere sixteen of the eighty-seven amtracs remained operational. The thirty-eight remaining amtracs, which had not been employed in the initial assault, were pre-loaded with critical combat supplies that had to be off-loaded before troops could be carried.

Easy Company Commander reported that he had already lost all of his officers and half his NCOs, many before they had even made it to the beach. Similar losses were experienced up and down the line. As bleak as the circumstances appeared, it seemed as if the marines had finally carved out a substantial beachhead, overrunning many Japanese gun turrets and pillboxes. One encouraging development was that a few medium tanks had made it ashore, along with some 75-mm pack howitzers, semi-portable weapons ideal for amphibious assaults. However, they still had no flamethrowers. Experience had taught the marines that positions reduced only with grenades could come alive again.

One of the squad leaders crawled within two feet of an enemy trench and tossed in a hand grenade, but the Japanese soldier tossed it back, the explosion wounding the marine. Thad and Joe Louis Boyd rushed to treat the wounded man. While Thad was removing the man's fatigue jacket so he could treat the shrapnel wounds in his back, Joe Louis Boyd peeked into the depression and spotted the enemy soldier and killed him. Another Japanese in the trench, unseen by Boyd who had his back to him, stood up and had begun to raise his rifle when Thad saw him, shouted at the big black man, managed to remove his .45 from its holster, and fired. It was a chest shot, center mass. The Jap fell back, still holding his rifle. His first kill. He felt absolutely nothing, having killed a man. He wondered if he should be feeling something.

The rest of the day was spent eliminating Japanese pillboxes, avoiding sniper fire, mortar and artillery fire, and generally trying to stay alive. The marines had a method for taking out the pillboxes. First they had to determine the field of fire for the individual machine gun, which meant how far right and left the Japanese could shoot. To do this, a marine would stand up, present himself as a target and immediately duck behind cover. He would draw fire, move to his right and keep moving until he no longer drew fire. Repeat the process, this time moving to his left, thereby establishing the effective field of fire. Then knowing that he couldn't be hit from that angle, another marine would charge the pillbox and shove a grenade through the small opening of the pillbox. The problem was that the entry hole was so small he could rarely toss a grenade that would kill both Japs, the gunner and loader. Sometimes the grenade would disable the gun, sometimes not.

It had been determined that Rat was the fastest man in the company. He claimed he could outrun any cop in the Bronx. He, perhaps reluctantly, volunteered to be the grenade tosser, while Hernandez, pretty quick himself, would be the duck in the shooting gallery. Thad watched them take out pillbox after pillbox, sometimes even laughing. Thad was thinking that these guys were just a little bit nuts and had more guts than a packing house.

This continued for the remainder of the day. They took out a pillbox and moved, if only for a few yards, while Thad did his best to treat the wounded. There were too many. Everywhere you looked there were fallen marines. All he could do was to go from one to another, take care of those that could be saved, give a hit of morphine to those in unimaginable pain, and say a little prayer for those lifeless, sometimes dismembered shapes, all the time wondering if this was the best he could do. He knew that if a severely wounded man received care within one hour after his injury, he faced a ninety-percent chance of survival. The odds plummeted to twenty-five percent after eight hours. After administering morphine or sulfa and stemming blood flows to stabilize a wounded marine, he would make a preliminary diagnosis of the injury for medical staff at an aid station a short distance from the front. Physicians at the aid station would dispense additional treatment, which might include surgery, before sending the wounded on to a hospital ship.

Late that afternoon Thad headed back to the aid station on the beach to replenish his medical kit. Enjoying the temporary lull from his duties, he looked toward the lagoon where men still struggled to make it to shore.

He used the lull to relax for a few minutes. He sat with his back to the seawall, while a lieutenant from another company faced him and offered Thad a cigarette. He accepted. He didn't have the habit yet, but he was working on it. Suddenly the lieutenant's face twisted with a surprised look. The man slumped forward, dead from a bullet that had passed just above Thad and gone directly into his forehead. Thad grabbed the lieutenant's carbine, spotted a sniper in a tree, cranked off a full magazine, and finally a body dropped out.

He kept the carbine, took seven full magazines from the lieutenant's now-lifeless form, and returned to his platoon.

7

Of the five thousand marines who crashed Betio's beaches that first day fifteen hundred were dead, wounded or missing by nightfall. The survivors clung to thin beachheads, weary, undermanned, and worried about survival.

With nightfall came the flares, flares and tracers, flares, tracers and doubt. After a full day of fighting and mounting losses, the marines had secured less than one quarter of the island. Vice Admiral Raymond Spruance, Commander Central Pacific Force who had been assigned the capture of Tarawa, received a message that first day: "Situation grave." The marine lines, such as they were, had gaps, some as large as six hundred yards. If the Japanese had mounted a counterattack that first night, the final outcome might have been different. All the marines could have done would be to set up a defense behind the seawall until they were overwhelmed and driven into the sea.

The attempt to land supplies and more marines during the night was becoming increasingly difficult, if not impossible. The Japanese had managed to set up machine guns on the pier as well as on the sunken freighter. They had snipers firing from the sunken and disabled landing crafts.

Fortunately, the counterattack never materialized. The Japanese matched the marines in sheer numbers, occupied stronger positions, and had the advantage of knowing the terrain better than their foe.

Shadowy figures moved through the night, eyes seeing thing things they really didn't see. Even though they had been issued orders to maintain strict silence, Willis emptied a clip into what he imagined to be a Jap, shouting, "I got him, Gunny!"

Joe Louis Boyd, in the crater with Willis, said, "Nice going. You just killed an oil drum." The use of firearms was discouraged. It was feared that the jumpy troops (Willis?) might accidentally shoot at American reinforcements being shuttled into the line. The men were told to instead use their bayonets against suspected infiltrators. Schedules were established. Two men to remain awake for every one that slept, or one man awake while his buddy slept.

Through the night, men heard cries for aid. "Come help me!" or "Help! I'm wounded!" but marines remained at their posts as ordered. No one was to move around in the darkness.

All night long, one group of men never ceased working. While the marines guarded the thin perimeter that defined the American controlled sliver of beach, Thad and the other corpsmen treated hundreds of wounded. Working out of seized pillboxes and bunkers, the corpsmen operated by flashlight and ignored snipers' bullets. Thad spent much of that first night braving enemy fire at the pier, where he made numerous trips carrying out wounded men and bringing back ammunition and water.

Marines who had been ripped apart by bullets and mangled by mortar fire patiently waited in shell holes outside the bunkers while Thad and other corpsmen worked on others. Back at the aid station, some faced painful operations performed by a naval physician. Even when his anesthesia supply ran out, few marines complained.

The Japanese failed to attack during that first crucial night because they lacked two necessary items—a commander and communications. Admiral Shibasaki had been killed in the initial bombardment. Their capable leader most assuredly would have ordered a counter attack. In his absence the command fell to less-capable, lower-ranked officers, and since the naval bombardment had destroyed the communications network connecting all segments of the garrison, they had no way of contacting each other and coordinating an assault.

Dawn of the second day found Captain Bartholomew lying flat on his back in a pool of blood at the entrance to a captured Japanese bunker. He was asleep, not dead. The blood came from one of the bunker's defenders. At midnight, exhausted after making another round checking his tiny perimeter, he finally gave out. He had dragged the corpse out of the bunker, lain down, and fallen asleep, unaware or uncaring of what he might by lying in. When Thad saw him he asked him if he was hurt, the captain being completely unaware of the blood covering the back of his utility jacket.

That morning, with the aid of tanks, air strikes, and naval bombardment, the entire western end of the island was secured. Finally, Colonel Shoup had what he so desperately needed: the opportunity to land reinforcements across a secure beachhead with full-unit integrity and supporting arms, if he could get them safely across the reef. *If.*

With the dawn came the Higgins boats, no amtracs. Low tide. The result was the same as the day before. Waves of Higgins boats approached the reef, while marines along the seawall stared in helpless fascination. Japanese gunners that had infiltrated the disabled amtracs and the sunken freighter opened up an unrelenting fire. They had re-occupied the pier and were firing from there. The horror had just begun. The big dual-purpose antiaircraft guns leveled their long barrels and began zeroing in on the Higgins boats themselves, waiting for the moment the craft slammed into the reef and began lowering its bow ramp. The boat would be blown completely out of the water. It was worse than it was on D-day. All hell had broken loose. A chaplain, agonizing over the loss of so many remarked, "Fire from enemy positions mowed them down as a scythe cuts through grass."

At the end, only courage enabled the survivors to struggle ashore against the hellish cross fire. One landing team had suffered over three hundred casualties. The unit had lost all its flame throwers, demolitions, and heavy weapons. Courage alone would not prevail against fortified positions.

Wounded marines clung to the reef or lay in the shallows. Others huddled in groups, demoralized and weaponless. Japanese snipers were picking them off, one by one.

Meanwhile, the hellish tide finally began to rise, and Higgins boats began retrieving the more critically wounded and taking them back to the transports. They would land more troops, then, on returning, pull more men out of the water.

As the morning wore on, bodies were drifting slowly in the reddish water just off the beach. There were destroyed amtracs and Higgins boats. The stench of decaying bodies covered the island like a cloud.

Thad, feeling secure in his bomb crater, remembered the last meal he had eaten: steak and eggs aboard ship the previous day. He broke open his K-ration carton: "RATION, TYPE K. BREAKFAST UNIT." it contained canned meat, biscuits, soluble coffee, a fruit bar, gum, sugar tablets, four cigarettes, water purification tablets, toilet paper, and a wooden spoon. "Ain't exactly steak and eggs." He popped open the canned meat with the little can opener that hung from his dog tag chain, was well into the canned meat and a biscuit, when for the first time that day, came the call. Corpsman!

The firing had not yet reached the intensity of yesterday but would surely reach it again today. Thad reached the fallen marine. The gunny was there kneeling beside him, Lieutenant Stanley, the prima donna. Thad noticed how flat the poncho laid over him, where his feet and legs should have been. The gunny followed his eyes and then nodded. "Both of 'em," he said, "above the knees."

"How?"

"Must have stepped on an unexploded mortar round or hand grenade. Set it off."

Squad leaders had applied tourniquets to both of his legs, and all Thad could do was give him a hit of morphine, hoping the Lieutenant would slip into the never-never land where there is no pain, no anything but sleep.

Lieutenant Stanley moved a little, opening his eyes and focusing on Thad. His eyes were a little fuzzy from the morphine. He seemed casual and at ease. He licked his lips once or twice before he spoke. First in a whisper, then grew stronger as he talked. He was fighting the effects of the morphine, knowing that if he went to sleep, he would surely die, never wake up.

He told Thad to tell Rat that he was giving him a battlefield promotion. Back to PFC. Was that a smile? With that, he closed his eyes and went to sleep.

He was simply a young man who had been handed a tough and dirty job to do, who had found out all he could about how to do it and had done it the best way he knew how.

When he told Rat about his promotion, Rat said, "Swell. While these promotions are being handed out, maybe I can be Platoon Leader for a day."

Suddenly came an unbelievable burst of fire. *Run! Take cover! Any crater will do!* Thad was in a frozen panic. Behind him, Wilson, one of the squad leaders said calmly, almost sleepily, "Hey, Doc, give me a hand, huh?"

Thad turned in the crater, careful not to raise his body, and crawled the inches to Wilson's face.

"I can't feel either leg. It's cold, man."

The sand was stained, and blood was oozing from the middle of his waist to his ankles. He unbuttoned Wilson's fatigue jacket to examine the wound. He couldn't hold back; he threw up his breakfast.

"Pretty bad, huh, Doc?" he whispered.

While Thad was preparing a morphine injection, Wilson coughed once. A gurgling cough. Twice, and died.

I'm not prepared for this.

More machine gun nests. More bunkers. Marines with flame throwers had finally made it to the beach during the night. Thad and Davis watched one, obviously working with another marine, charge a bunker with his flame thrower while the other man drew fire. A steady burst of flame through the gun port. Screaming, a Jap ran out of the bunker, swatting at the flames that engulfed his body and rolling on the ground. The other marine, the one that had been drawing fire, shot and killed him.

Davis said, "Shoulda let him cook."

Thad figured these guys might as well have a bull's eye painted on their backs. What if a bullet hits the damn tank? He had heard also that guys packing a radio on their backs were also prime targets.

Throughout the day marines leaped into foxholes, craters, and emplacements, and bayoneted the enemy or shot them. There was a lot of bayoneting.

Boudreau jumped into a foxhole, plunged his bayonet into an enemy, while keeping one eye out for other Japanese soldiers who might approach while he bayoneted the defender. It happened. While he was trying to remove his bayonet from the first, he grabbed his K-BAR and killed the second opponent. When he was joined by the gunny, he said "*Bonjour*, Gunny. *Je faites bon*, huh?"

Later that day, Thad, Boudreau, and the gunny came upon a bomb crater with four corpses leaning against the craters walls. Two rested together, the other two were lying separately. There was a foot gone on one of them, with the beginnings of a tourniquet on the leg, the second corpse dead lying on top of the foot. Another had his head blown apart. Weapons and parts of uniforms were gone. Souvenirs. All that remained were bodies.

Thad looked closely at them. They were short haired and thin. The flies had found them and swarmed around the wounds looking for egg nests. And the stench. *The whole island smells like death.*

By now marines had attacked across the island, thereby cutting the island in two. Momentum had moved to the Americans, but the position was tenuous. The Japanese counterattacked viciously, but the tide of battle was finally beginning to shift toward the Americans as the afternoon wore on. The fighting was still intense, the Japanese fire was still murderous, but the surviving marines were on the move, no longer gridlocked on the beach, and they were well supported by artillery and naval guns.

Optimism came from different sources. Marines moving through Japanese defenders noticed that Japanese defenders, instead of fighting, had started to commit suicide. They counted seventeen Japanese bodies in one bunker, all dead from self-inflicted wounds. Shoup took this as a sign that the Japanese spirit had been broken.

At 1600 that afternoon Shoup sent a situation report to Julian Smith: "Casualties: many. Percentage dead: unknown. Combat efficiency: We are winning."

8

Rat and Hernandez, the company's two bunker busters, were sharing a crater when Hernandez spotted a Japanese soldier in a coconut tree drawing a direct bead on him. Hernandez realized he had to shoot first before the enemy sniper shot him. He and Rat fired in unison, killing the sniper, but not before Hernandez was hit, the round grazing the top of his helmet. Made his ears ring. The dead sniper, tied to the tree, hung there like a shot squirrel hung up in the branches.

The afternoon of that second day, Thad treated a marine from another platoon who was lying on his stomach with one foot twisted skyward. He thought the man had a broken leg and turned him over. He put his hand where the marine's leg should have been. His leg was blown off. He had grabbed a handful of blood, tendons and bone.

Once again, he fought the urge to vomit. He applied a tourniquet to the upper portion of the leg to stem the blood flow, then administered a shot of morphine to dull the pain. He didn't have the heart to tell the obviously dying marine how serious the injury was, so he told him he had a broken leg.

Then there were the others. The ones he could treat. The quiet courage of the marines impressed him. There was no panic. They'd say, "Thanks, Doc," then get up and resume fighting. These were the men that kept him going, thinking that maybe he was doing some good after all. He knew that he could be killed or wounded as he bent over to treat a man, but he had a job to do and never dwelt on being maimed or killed. Never gave it a thought. Just did what he was trained to do.

Captain Bartholomew asked for a volunteer to cross the airfield and scout the enemy's defenses. A lieutenant from another platoon volunteered, and agreed to signal when he felt it was safe for the rest of the company to join him.

He dashed across the runway without drawing fire, but when he reached the opposite beach, a bullet grazed his mouth and knocked out his upper front teeth. Stunned, but still conscious, he tossed a grenade into the bunker, killing the occupants, then signaled to Captain Bartholomew across the airstrip that it was safe to cross.

Captain Bartholomew stood up and said, "Let's go, boys." The riflemen ran across first, then provided cover for the machine gunners. Thad was among the last to cross, the thinking was that if any of the marines were hit, he might be able to render aid or at least with help, drag the injured to safety. It wasn't necessary. The marines had reached their destination without suffering a single casualty. As most Japanese defenses in this area faced the ocean rather than the airstrip, the marines had advanced before the Japanese had time to react and man inland defenses.

The marines had finally made it across the airfield to the opposite side of the island. Thad thought, *From sea to shining sea. Now what?* The company was occupying a one-hundred-yard tank trap. Captain Bartholomew said he needed two volunteers to re-cross the airfield, pick up ammunition at the beach, then bring it back to the trench. No one budged. Thad thought, *He's got to be kidding, right?* The captain was asking his men to twice retrace the steps they had just taken. They were lucky the first time, but to do it two more times?

Finally, Roy Boy and a redheaded boy named Fredrickson, the one they called Booger Red, volunteered. Roy Boy later explained, "That's the stupidest thing I've ever done." He and Booger Red shed all of their equipment except for their rifles and ammunition and took off.

A Japanese machine gun opened up on them within seconds. Bullets splattered into the ground as the pair dodged from hole to hole, keeping as low as possible.

When the pair finally arrived near the pier, Fredrickson stated, "I couldn't believe my eyes at the masses of bodies lying all along the beach as far as we could see. Hundreds and hundreds, most of them dead, some already bloated and stinking from the blazing-hot tropical sun."

After loading four ammunition belts apiece, which they crisscrossed across their shoulders, the two marines again darted from hole to hole, seemingly racing a stream of bullets as they ran across open territory. They fell into a deep bomb crater, occupied by a dead Jap, threw him out, and out of breath, leaned against the crater wall. Roy Boy spotted a coconut dangling from a tree beside them. He shot it down, cracked it open with his rifle butt and K-BAR, and in the middle of the battle, he and Booger Red enjoyed a refreshing drink of coconut milk. Thus energized, they made the final sprint across the airfield, and thanks to the poor shooting of the Jap machine gunner, reported to Captain Bartholomew.

Along with sulfa and plasma, a third medication, medicinal brandy, was used to alleviate the pain and discomfort of suffering marines. The quantities of brandy on hand did little to improve a wound or broken leg, but physicians and corpsmen noticed how an ounce or two of the alcohol improved the men's outlook. One official report after the battle conclude that while "The therapeutic value of brandy was not demonstrated…there is no question of its value as a morale factor."

Julian Smith sensed that Shoup, having run the show ashore for the first critical thirty-six hours, was now in over his head. By late D+1, however, eight infantry and two artillery batteries had been deployed. Early on D+2, virtually all the combat and support elements of the Second Marine Division would be deployed. It was time to send in the Chief of Staff, Colonel Merritt A. "Red Mike" Edson, hero of Guadalcanal.

Red Mike Edson reached Shoup's Command Post (CP) by 2030 and found the barrel-chested junior colonel still on his feet, grimy and haggard but full of fight. Edson assumed command, and though his role in the operation had ended, Shoup agreed to stay and help Edson formulate the next day's offensive.

Shoup had no grounds to object to Edson's assumption of command and willingly shared his knowledge of the battlefield with the chief of staff. In Shoup's eyes it probably helped that Edson was a proven combat warrior. Earlier, however, Shoup had resisted being relieved by senior officers. The first occurred during the night of D-Day when a general reached the pier head. Shoup bluntly told the general not to come ashore, that there was no place to land. This was stretching the truth just a tad. Artillerymen were filing ashore along the pier all through the night, unscathed. He finally told the general, "Get out from under that pier" and "go out and get in communications with the division."

Explaining the fluid tactical situation ashore to Edson took Shoup several hours. As Edson formulated his attack plan for the third day exhausted marines fell into their foxholes for the second night, looking forward to catching more sleep than on the first night. The Japanese had not counterattacked when they expected them to, so possibly a quiet second night could be expected.

9

On the third morning, a bulldozer was busy scooping a long trench, three feet deep, that would serve as a temporary cemetery for the marines whose bodies were gently placed side by side in a long row. A burial party was collecting the dead, many of whom had been floating in the lagoon for two days.

The flow of supplies had increased and these were streaming in along the pier. Additional tanks, flamethrowers, and armored half-tracks could now support the offensive against a Japanese opponent whose numbers and fighting capability diminished by the hour. American material superiority was overwhelming the spirited but outclassed foe.

The morning was spent assaulting Japanese positions that had been troubling the marines for two days. Two of the pesky fortifications were subdued by a suppressing fire laid down by a company of marines, and a tank pumped several rounds into the steel pillbox's opening from point-blank range. Then marines rushed forward and destroyed the position with grenades and demolition charges.

The toughest obstacle would be the bombproof shelter farther inland. Japanese machine gunners sat in protected holes on the shelters top, while other gunners fired through narrow openings, waiting to repulse any Marine unit before it reached the slopes. Blasts from howitzers and tanks had been ineffectual, due to the layer of soft sand that muffled every explosion, and the Navy's destroyers could not chance a bombardment because the marines had crowded so close to the shelter. Navy dive bombers could perhaps do the trick, but this was out of the question for the same reason.

The plan was for Marine riflemen to pin down the Japanese with suppressing fire while the engineers and flamethrowers crept toward the bunker's top to destroy the machine-gun nests. With that opposition removed, the marines could then pour gasoline and throw hand grenades down the air vents to force the Japanese into the open, where they could be cut down by the marines.

Finally, with everyone in place, a company of marines laid down suppressing fire while thirty to forty men stormed the slopes. The engineers were waved to the top, covered by flamethrowers roasting machine gunners, while a short-fused TNT charge was placed in the middle of the crest. The explosion and dust provided enough distraction for engineers to make it to the top.

The bunker was destroyed by the engineers dropping TNT down the air vents. Elements of four marine companies now surrounded the location to cut off any retreat and to guard a bulldozer that slowly moved up to shove sand into any openings and seal any Japanese inside.

More than one hundred Japanese defenders poured out of an exit to the bunker to evade certain death from fire and explosion, only to be slaughtered by the marines posted outside.

By dusk the third day, the marines had finally seized the upper hand. The Japanese still fought in two places: the system of defenses in the "Pocket," and an estimated one thousand

Japanese gathering at the tail end of Betio. All that remained for the next day, hopefully the last, was to wipe out these two isolated locations.

The battalion manned positions on the front line between the airfield and the southern shore. If a Japanese attack was coming, it would be coming from those Japanese boxed in on the tail end of the island. Thad and Rat, sharing a foxhole, hoped against hope that this night would be as quiet as the first two. It was not to be.

The first of four counterattacks came at 7:30, when Japanese soldiers with fixed bayonets rushed through thick vegetation toward the marine lines. Japanese officers waved swords while soldiers fired from the hip as they ran.

The Japanese had to advance through a five-hundred-yard artillery curtain to reach the marines. Many died in the punishing bombardment, which came within seventy-five yards of Thad and the other marines, but plenty still managed to filter through to the marine lines.

Rat had his bayonet fixed, while Thad, with the carbine he'd taken from the dead lieutenant and his .45, prepared to defend their little patch of the island from this screaming hoard of Japanese rushing toward them. Rat adjusted his steel-rimmed glasses and asked, "You ready, Doc?"

"Ready as I'll ever be, I guess." He was thinking, *How can anyone possibly ever be ready for what's about to happen?*

Marines greeted the invaders with their own bayonets, then engaged in bitter hand-to-hand combat. They clutched each other's throats, bit, gouged, and kicked one another.

Thad and Rat were firing and reloading, when a screaming Japanese soldier managed to jump into their foxhole. Rat bayoneted the man in the stomach and fired a round into him at the same time and freed his bayonet. The Jap was obviously dead, but Thad put a round into his head just to be sure. They moved the body to the front between them and the onrushing Japanese, laid their weapons across him and continued to fire. Soon another leaped at them, and Thad clubbed him to death with the butt of his carbine.

After two hours of a melee of grenade throwing, machine gunning and bayoneting, the bloody combat ended. In some spots, to the marines' front, bodies were piled three and four feet deep. Thad and Rat prepared for a long night. As much as they hoped for an end, they guessed the Japanese would return before long.

The lull didn't even last for an hour and a half. At 11:00 a second assault hit the marine lines. The Japanese tried to intimidate their opponents by screaming, "Marine, you die!" and "Japanese drink marines' blood!"

The ever-cool Rat said, "Ain't they something?"

Japanese armed only with knives or bayonets leaped into foxholes and again grappled hand-to-hand with the marines. A Japanese, clutching a grenade with the pin drawn, jumped into a foxhole with Davis, killing Davis and himself. Tall, good looking, shy James Davis, his upper torso a bloody mess, his once-handsome face unrecognizable.

Lieutenant Pond, "Duck" to his friends, Lieutenant Stanley's replacement, reached for the field telephone in the midst of the counterattack to call down artillery when a huge (they weren't all small), Japanese jumped into his foxhole. The lieutenant dodged the long bayonet aimed at his stomach, grabbed the soldier's weapon, finally managing to take it away from him, and clubbed the big Jap to death with his own rifle. He shot him in the head, just to be sure, and threw him out of the foxhole. The new platoon leader was going to be okay.

Meanwhile, two Japanese soldiers jumped toward Thad and Rat. The first lunged at Rat with his bayonet. He reached up with his left hand and grabbed the bayonet. His palm was sliced, and the Jap managed to stick him in the right shoulder, but not deep.

They struggled for maybe a minute, rolling around, Rat trying to get out of the way of the bayonet. He held him off until Thad, having disposed of the second Jap with several rounds from his carbine, took his .45, shoved it into the face of Rat's opponent, and pulled the trigger. The round went into the left eye of the soldier and came out the side of his head, missing Rat by inches.

For a time, it looked like the marines were going to be overrun. "We are killing them as fast as they come at us, but we can't hold much longer; we need reinforcements!" shouted Captain Bartholomew over the phone.

The reply was, "We haven't got them to send to you. You've got to hold."

After putting down the field telephone, he said, more to himself than anyone in particular, "If we don't hold we may lose the entire battalion."

For thirty minutes a destroyer shelled fifty yards ahead of the marine lines, dangerously close, while artillery trained their guns on the Japanese. That, along with the courage of the individual marines, finally halted the second attack.

Between that attack and the third, which was sure to come, Thad patched up the Rat. Sufficient light was no problem, thanks to the flares which at times lit up the battlefield like daylight. He wrapped his hand, sprinkled sulfa powder into the shoulder wound, which had stopped bleeding, and applied a field dressing. Thad asked him if he didn't want to go back to the aid station at the beach for better treatment. Rat said he'd rather stick it out.

"Your call."

At 3:A.M. they came again. The Japanese opened fire with machine guns from demolished trucks about fifty yards in front. A unit of marines crawled into the darkness, destroyed the guns, and ended what was the briefest assault of the night.

One hour later the Japanese returned in force with more than four hundred soldiers. They had unleashed a last-gasp attempt to overwhelm the marines. A failure for the Japanese here meant abandoning hopes of holding on to Betio.

Again armed with machine guns, rifles, bayonets, grenades, rifles, and swords, the Japanese, some wearing only loincloths, swarmed toward the marines in a do-or-die assault. Heavy marine gunfire cut swaths into the Japanese ranks. Tracers crisscrossed the battlefield. Yellow streams poured out of the Japanese weapons, red, white, or pink from the marines. Offshore, two destroyers emptied their five-inch magazines into the charging Japanese.

Once again, combat became uncivilized, as men, many out of ammunition from the earlier charges, resorted to hands and clubs. The initial Japanese charges maintained a semblance of order, but this final attack turned into an all-out suicidal, banzai onslaught.

Hernandez heard Joe Louis Boyd cry for help. He grabbed his bayonet, killed the enemy soldier threatening Boyd, then bayoneted three other Japanese soldiers as they ran at him one by one. As he yanked his bayonet out of the fourth man, a Japanese officer ran a saber through his back and killed him.

Finally, around 5 A.M., the attack ceased. As many as five hundred Japanese bodies littered the territory immediately in front of marine lines. The First Battalion saw its ranks depleted by three hundred dead and wounded. Captain Bartholomew praised his men for staging such a valiant defense. "Every one of you is a champion."

Such tactics as banzai attacks are typically regarded as a suicidal headlong charge by poorly armed, sake-soused fanatics seeking a quick and honorable death. Not these. The attacks on Betio were intelligently planned and professionally executed.

The nighttime counterattacks proved to be the final gasp for the Japanese on Betio. After the marines repulse those four charges, two areas remained to be cleared, the Pocket in the west and the remnants hemmed into the tail in the east. Both were eliminated by the early afternoon of November 23.

Two units closed in on the Pocket. They advanced in a semicircle, converged at the airfield, and trapped the Japanese in a rapidly dwindling area along the beach. Supported by 75-mm guns, marines quickly destroyed the set of pillboxes from which so many of their brothers had been killed and declared the western half of Betio secured at 1:05 P.M.

As for the remaining enemy at the tail, supported by tanks, a battalion jumped off at 8:00 A.M. They encountered minimal opposition until they moved east of the airfield, where a set of pillboxes and bunkers slowed the momentum. One company of marines swerved around the Japanese flank, while another attacked from the front, causing seventy-five Japanese soldiers to rush into the open. From point-blank range, a tank turned her guns on the fleeing soldiers, and the ensuing massacre ended the confrontation and enabled the battalion to continue toward the tail.

Japanese resistance had obviously lessened. marines encountered fewer interlocking fields of fire along the way, which simplified the tasked of the flamethrowers and demolitions men destroying pillboxes. As the Japanese retreated toward the narrow east end of Betio, naval gunfire tore into their ranks from offshore, while the marines blocked any possible escape route. The Japanese were trapped in a constantly shrinking area.

By this time, the marines were in no mood to take prisoners. The savagery and blood, the fear and worry, the loss of friends shattered whatever civilized behavior that the young men took to the battlefield. At this point they didn't even try to take prisoners.

At 1:00 P.M., for the first time since D-Day, the marines controlled the island from end to end, and the guns fell silent. At

1:05, Julian Smith sent a message to Admiral Hill, Commander Fifth Amphibious Force: "Betio has fallen." After seventy-six hours of practically non-stop bloodshed—combat rarely matched elsewhere for savagery—the marines had taken the two-mile-long plot of land in the Central Pacific.

The initial wounded had been evacuated during the first day, when corpsmen placed them on rubber boats, and marines pulled them to the reef. Landing craft then ferried them to transports, where surgeons performed operations and readied them for the long trip to Hawaiian hospitals. Now on the fourth day, the flow of wounded continued. While Thad was helping one of the wounded marines into a rubber boat, from somewhere behind him, he heard the voice, "*Bon l'apres-midi*, Doc Hayes." And there he was, lying on a stretcher, smiling.

Thad didn't know if he was stoned on morphine or not, because the Cajun was always smiling. "Boudreau, you crazy bastard! What happened?"

"Last night I was in my foxhole, minding my own business, I think it was last night, shooting at these screaming people running at me, when I felt something tear into my leg that somehow turned me upside down. I was lying on my back, trying to see what was wrong with my leg, that seemed to be turned in the wrong direction, when this little son of a bitch jumps into the foxhole with me, and damned if he doesn't stick me in the other leg with his bayonet. Booger Red, who was in the foxhole with me, shot this guy several times, I think. Red tied off both legs to stop the bleeding, and as soon as the shooting stopped, a doc from another company gave me a shot that made all the hurt go away, and had me delivered here to the beach. And now they're going to load me into one of those little rubber boats and take me away. Maybe back to Lafayette. '*Allons a Lafayette.*' What do you think?"

He's stoned. "I think the little rubber boat is going to take you out to one of those ships, and the ship will take you as far as Hawaii. You'll have to get to Lafayette on your own."

Boudreau's left leg was in a splint, had been straightened out as far as Thad could tell, and his right trouser leg had been cut off. The bayonet wound was heavily bandaged. Boudreau was going to be just fine.

As he was being lifted into the boat, Thad took his hand and told him he'd see him in Hawaii.

"*Voir vois plus tard. Faire attention,* Doc."

They pushed the little rubber boat out into the water. Thad thought he heard singing. Couldn't be, but there it was: *"Jole Blon, ma chere, 'tit fille."*

"Just might give myself a shot."

On 24 November, the day after the fighting at Betio ended, marines proudly hauled two flags to the tops of palm trees, both denuded of fronds from the battle. The Stars and Stripes on one and, as Tarawa had been a British possession before the war, the Union Jack on the other.

A bugle sounded and deeply moved men who, only hours before, had been scratching and clawing for this little plot of dirt. Men turned from digging foxholes, from unloading boats, from burying the dead. They stood at attention, saluting with their dirty, tired, young hands. Some of the wounded managed to stand up, too, while the more seriously hurt could only turn their heads as they lay on their stretchers.

With marines looking up and seeing the Stars and Stripes snapping in the breeze, Betio at last belonged to the Corps. They had fought and killed and maimed for precisely this moment. They could hold their heads high knowing they had triumphed on a nightmarish battlefield.

10

With the capture of Betio, there was still work to be done: the capture of the rest of the islands in Tarawa atoll. The battalion assigned this task, Second Battalion, Sixth Marines, started its long march up the atoll on 24 November.

Even before that, however, some preliminary reconnaissance work had been done on the little islets, east of Betio by the division's scout company. While the battle raged on Betio, it was assigned the mission of reconnoitering these unnamed islets.

On 21 November, a platoon landed on the first island where it found fuel dumps, bomb and mine dumps, but no Japanese. Another platoon on the next island located a Japanese position, estimated to contain one hundred of the enemy, and a radio station. Another platoon, a little further up the atoll captured one Japanese laborer and several natives.

Second Battalion, Sixth Marines, L/T (Landing Team) 2/6, embarked on boats from Betio at 0500, 24 November and moved to the first of the islets to begin the trek to the north. By nightfall, the battalion had passed through several native villages recently evacuated. No enemy force was contacted.

The march was resumed on 25 November and at the end of

the day the battalion was well up the atoll. Still no contact with the enemy had been made. By late afternoon of 26 November, L/T 2/6 had reached the south end of the last large island at the northwest end of Tarawa atoll. Before bivouacking for the night, a company was sent northwest to maintain position as an advance covering force. The landing team knew from information received from the scouts that somewhere north of them there were at least one hundred Japanese.

This was verified when patrols ran into Japanese patrols at sunset. A brief firefight ensued, in which two marines were wounded, and it was believed that two or three Japanese were killed. After dark, the patrol returned, and the company remained in its defensive position during the night. Occasional harassing enemy fire was received, but the marines held their fire and waited for daylight. There were no additional Marine casualties.

Next morning the landing team advanced with two companies in assault and one in reserve. Shortly after moving out they found the enemy position. Although the Japanese had no organized line, it was difficult to destroy them. Broken into small groups, each of which was in a pit or behind coconut logs, the enemy held their fire until the marines were nearly on top of them. Vegetation was dense, and the fighting was at close range.

After several hours of typical jungle fighting, the main enemy resistance was overcome, and L/T 2/6 returned to mopping up and patrolling. The day's action cost three officers killed and one wounded; enlisted losses amounted to twenty-nine killed and fifty-eight wounded. One hundred and seventy-five Japanese were killed, and two Korean laborers captured.

One tiny islet remained to be taken. It was found to contain no Japanese, and by 0800 on the morning of 28 November the capture of Tarawa atoll was complete.

The battle for Bloody Tarawa was over. Mission

accomplished, but the marines paid dearly for this little scrap of land in the Central Pacific. General Shoup later recalled the savage desperate fighting and wondered "why two nations would spend so much for so little." Nearly six thousand Japanese and Americans died on the tiny island in seventy-six hours of fighting.

Julian Smith summed up the lessons learned at Tarawa by commenting, "We made fewer mistakes than the Japs did."

11
Camp Tarawa, Waimea, Hawaii
December 1943

The remnants of the proud Second Marine Division, the heroes of Tarawa had come to Waimea to rest from the bloodiest battle in the history of the Marine Corps, to replace the dead and wounded, and to prepare for crucial battles that lay ahead.

The big man was not from Waimea. Everyone from Hayashi Store knew that, but he was not Army either; they had departed some weeks before. He had on a government-issue T-shirt and dark-green pants without pockets in the back.

"Do you have clothes? I need clothes," he said as he reached into his pocket for money. Behind him, were other marines in various levels of undress, not like soldiers that had been in town the previous year. Quickly, the Hayashi Store sold all its clothes and blankets to the shivering men. Later marines wandered around town, cursing the wind that wasn't supposed to have been part of their trip to paradise.

The tents had been left by the Army stacked in the pasture and had to be set up. More critical was the lack of sleeping bags and blankets. Some bureaucrat had expected the marines to come prepared. He apparently decided that each marine had been issued blankets and sleeping bags along with complete uniforms and would be prepared for the Waimea winter.

The division had come directly from its victory at Tarawa. Much of the equipment had been lost in the battle. Men had stripped off their clothing and rid themselves of the horrible smell of Betio. Aboard transports on their way to Waimea, they made do with pieces of clothing that they might have stuck in their packs or borrowed clothing from the ship's crew, having returned it when they debarked, expecting to be issued new uniforms when they arrived. It was not to be. It would be days before fresh uniforms found their way to the raggedy bunch of heroes.

The marines had shipped directly to Oahu, where they left their wounded for treatment. Then on the Big Island they were loaded into trucks or boarded trains for the cold journey to Waimea in the northern, mountainous area of the Big Island.

After getting the tents set up and finally being issued clothing, the Second marine Division, what was left of it, began the process of healing. They had sustained over three thousand casualties, and these men would have to be replaced. Charlie Company had lost over one quarter of the men that landed on Betio. From the First Platoon, Davis, Hernandez, and Lieutenant Stanley were dead. Thirteen others had sustained wounds.

Except for his nerves, Thad escaped relatively unscathed. He jumped at the sound of any sudden noise, as did the rest of the survivors, and the smell of death seemed to linger. He was exhausted and had trouble sleeping. Some would get on crying jags. Others seemed to be talking to themselves or to people that weren't there. They needed time—time to get well so they could go out and do it again.

The mail had caught up with them, and Thad had several letters from Lou Ann, a few from his parents, and one from Dolores, the girl he had met in New Zealand. He opened Lou Ann's first. She had started her sophomore year at Texas Women's University. She missed him. Hoped he was well. She had read in the newspapers and saw pictures in Life magazine of the horrible battle at a place called Tarawa, and hoped that he hadn't been there. The girls here dated boys from TCU, but she was remaining faithful, and hoped that he was. (Ha, ha.) She still didn't understand why he had joined the Navy and was with the Marines. "Shouldn't you be on a boat somewhere? You parents are fine, and Josie is engaged to a dentist from Odessa." The usual, "Love and kisses, I miss you, stay safe, and hurry home."

Dolores' letter: "How are you? I enjoyed our time together. It's awfully quiet since you marines left. Hope you are well. If you're ever back in New Zealand…" She went on to say that Margaret was in love with Jimmy, and they had talked about getting married when this terrible war is over.

Oh, man. He knew Davis liked her a lot, but Davis never talked to him about getting married to her. He was going to have to write her and tell her that Jimmy had been killed. But not today. First he'd write Lou Ann and his parents and think about how to break the news to Margaret, or maybe let Dolores tell her. He collected Davis' mail. Several were from Margaret. He'd have to return them. Right now he didn't want to think about it.

The first few weeks there was very little training and a lot of free time. There were movies and trips into town where they hit the bars. Their pockets were full from collecting back pay, and they didn't hesitate to spend it. Thad bought two kimonos, one for Lou Ann and one for Josie. He couldn't imagine his mother in a kimono. Some would give the clerk at the store all of their money and tell her they wanted good presents. Others sent money home. A few decided to save all their money so they could buy a car when they got back to the states, but most spent, and the Waimea merchants weren't about to object.

There was recreation. Word got around that there was going to be a baseball game—not your every day, run-of-the-mill baseball game, but a donkey baseball game. "What the hell is a donkey baseball game?"

Roy Boy knew. He had seen one played back home in Georgia. "Here's the deal," said Roy Boy: "The pitcher and the catcher are the only players not on a donkey. They remain afoot. You're sitting on your donkey, and you stay up there swinging until you hit the ball, which you will eventually do, because there ain't no such thing as ball and strikes. Then you and your donkey take off running toward first base. Just like real baseball.

"When you're in the field and the ball is hit toward you, you got to ride over to where the ball is, get off your donkey, pick up the ball, get back on your donkey, and ride it on in till you get close enough to make a throw to the infielder, sitting on his donkey, and nail the base runner. Donkey runner? Donkey rider? Don't matter. Nothing to it."

"What if the jackass don't want to go to first base?"

"You got to convince him that he wants to. You could hit him with your bat, but that would get you kicked out of the game, besides really upsetting the donkey, and these people are pretty particular about their donkeys. You got to talk to him. He'll listen."

"And if he ain't a good listener?"

"You'll think of something."

And the game was on. The Charlie Company Bad Asses vs. The Dog Company Do Gooders. Good vs. Evil. On the mound for the Bad Asses was Captain Bartholomew. Catching was Sergeant Bradley. The eleven donkeys were named after The

Seven Dwarfs plus Snow White. The remaining three were named Larry, Curley, and Moe.

First up was Roy Boy, since he was the only one that knew what the hell was going on. He took five pitches, swung at nine before smacking one between the third baseman and shortstop. He got his donkey aimed toward first base, and what do you know? The donkey trotted on down to first and keeps on trotting all the way to right field where he finally stopped to graze on the long, outfield grass.

Meanwhile the left fielder was trying to get his donkey moving so he could fetch the ball. Finally he got him motivated, jumped off, picked up the ball, climbed back on, and his donkey decided he wasn't going nowhere. The outfielder, after much prodding and cussing, finally gave up and threw the ball in the direction of first base. The first baseman happened to have a donkey, named Sneezy, that played by the rules. He trotted over to the ball. The first baseman climbed off and picked it up. Gunny was shouting at Roy Boy, still out in right field trying to get his animal to knock off the grazing. "Get your ass back here!" The first baseman aboard Sneezy trotted back to first base and Roy Boy was called out.

There was some excitement when Rat got a hit, couldn't get his donkey to move, climbed off and punched him square in the nose. The donkey, obviously offended, probably Grumpy, tried to bite Rat. Rat raised his bat like he was going to smack the donkey square in the head, dropped his bat and said, "I quit."

And so it went. The game was finally called because of darkness with Evil defeating Good two to one.

Then there was a rodeo. Since Thad was from Texas, it was naturally assumed that he was a cowboy. His friends entered him it the bareback event. Against his better judgment, he climbed on a little horse named Thunder or Lightning, he wasn't sure which. They opened the gate, and there they went. The rules said you had to hold on with one hand, but Thad figured, *Screw that*, and after a few jumps grabbed on with both hands. About halfway down the arena, he was leaning, finally riding perpendicular to the little horse. He could hear the whooping and hollering by his buddies in the stands as he bounced by. He finally had to let go, ending up underneath Thunder. Or Lightning. Somehow, he avoided getting stepped on. His friends clapped him on the back, bought him a beer, and told him that as a cowboy, he stunk.

The recreation helped. They could finally think about something other than the recent horrors, and eventually they began training once again. Thad had written Margaret, getting her address from one of the letters she had written Davis before returning them, and told her that Jimmy had been killed on Betio. He said he didn't suffer, was killed instantly. Even though Davis had never talked about it, Thad told her that he was looking forward to returning to New Zealand and marrying her. He said he talked about her all the time. In this case he might as well lie a little.

In late June, Boudreau rejoined the company, still his happy coon-ass self, his legs mended. He said his stay in the hospital in Hawaii was *merevilleux*.

After spending almost eight months in Waimea, the Battalion Commander told them that the First Marine Division needed a battalion to hold in reserve, but don't count on it. We're "battle tested," and that makes us "The Chosen."

Thad figured, *Chosen's ass. More like drawing the black bean.*

In August they climbed aboard trucks and trains and made their way back to the coast, where they boarded transports to join the invasion force now forming up in the Central Pacific. This time they were headed for an island called Peleliu, much larger than Betio, but surely it couldn't be as bad as that little stinking island. Could it?

Peleliu

The American assault on Peleliu, in the Palau Islands, had the highest casualty rate of any amphibious invasion in terms of men and material in the entire war. In the Pacific, Peleliu, shaped like a lobster claw if you used your imagination, was viewed as a potential threat to General Douglas MacArthur's invasion of the Philippines; its airfield would enable Japanese planes to strike at American landing and support ships as well as troops on the ground in the Philippines. Clearly, from MacArthur's perspective, the almost 11,000 man garrison on Peleliu had to be eliminated before his forces could move, unhindered, on his primary target, the Philippines. Thus the strategic legitimacy of the Peleliu operation was established. American amphibious doctrine—well developed and tested—was up to the task. The First Marine Division was ready. Peleliu, however proved to be quite different from the many previous battles in several fundamental ways, and would end with a high death toll, questionable strategic gain, and yet valuable insights for future operations.

Admiral Nimitz, Pacific Fleet Commander, ordered the invasion to take place on 15 September 1944. American amphibious doctrine had been refined and improved upon over a year of hard fighting, beginning with Tarawa, and was approaching the efficiency of a well-oiled machine by late 1944. Land-based targets would be destroyed by massive naval bombardment, lasting days, and the landings themselves would be immediately preceded by strafing and bombing runs by carrier-based aircraft. The troops would be carried to shore in successive waves, massing on the beaches until they had sufficient force to push inland. The shallow Japanese defenses, although held with vigor, would eventually be overwhelmed, and the marines would move and capture the island.

Only two minutes off schedule, on 15 September 1944, the first troops began landing at 0832, with the First Marine Regiment on the far left, Fifth Marines in the middle, and the Seventh Marines on the right (southern) end of the beaches. The regiments on the flanks were to move inland and wheel outward, while the Fifth Marines were to push across the airfield to the eastern side of the island. Should this be accomplished as planned, the entire southern end of the island—better than half the land mass—would be in American hands, and the rest of the operation would be over quickly. Major General William H. Rupertus, the First Marine Division Commander, apparently brimming with confidence in his men and himself, declared that Peleliu would be taken in only a few days. Hold that thought, Rup.

The Japanese, during the Navy's bombardment, had hunkered down in their caves, pillboxes, and trenches. They waited out the preliminary shellings and then assumed their well-protected, well-hidden positions. Compared to earlier island assaults, few Japanese were positioned directly opposite the beaches. Most were just inland, dug in, on the flanks of the beaches, and in the steep mountains immediately north of the airfield. Consequently, the vast majority of positions remained unscathed as of D-Day. The enemy troops, while demonstrating a great deal of fire discipline, still managed to inflict heavy damage on the landing crafts.

Major General Rupert's three-day war lasted more than two months, costing over 12,000 lives on both sides. The First Marine Division was severely mauled by casualties on Peleliu and remained out of action until the invasion of Okinawa on April 1, 1945.

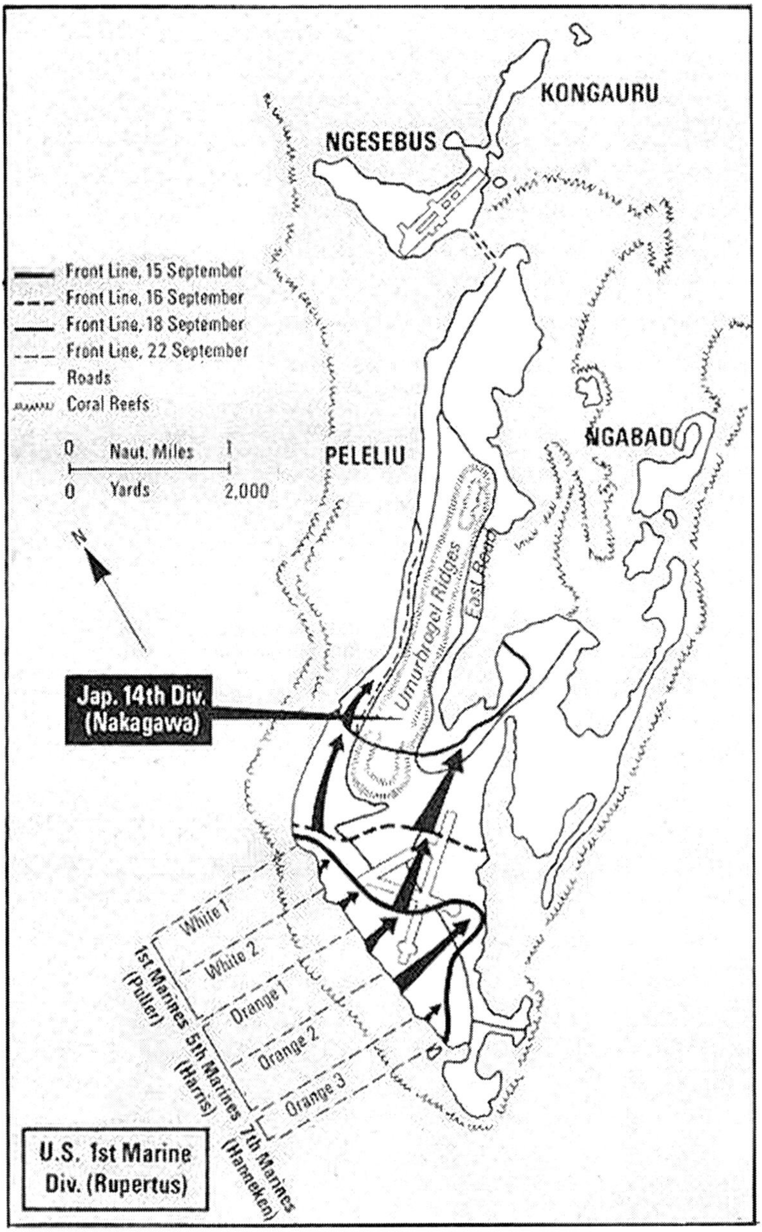
KONGAURU
NGESEBUS
Front Line, 15 September
Front Line, 16 September
Front Line, 18 September
Front Line, 22 September
Roads
Coral Reefs
0 Naut. Miles 1
0 Yards 2,000
N
PELELIU
NGABAD
Umurbrogol Ridges
East Road
Jap. 14th Div. (Nakagawa)
White 1
White 2
Orange 1
Orange 2
Orange 3
1st Marines (Puller)
5th Marines (Harris)
7th Marines (Hanneken)
U.S. 1st Marine Div. (Rupertus)

12
15 September 1944

From the amphibious tractor, Thad got his first look at the beach. The big guns from the Navy ships, miles behind them, were blasting the island. The huge shells tore overhead, roaring like locomotives. Huge geysers of water rose around the amtracs as they approached the reef. The beach was now marked along its length by fires and a thick wall of smoke. Navy Dauntless dive bombers made their bombing runs, and Hellcat fighters strafed targets, both real and imagined. The smoke was so thick there was no way they could identify individual targets.

Thad, hanging over the side of the amtrac, could see that some of the landing crafts had made it to the beach. Marines were pouring out, running, falling. One of the amtracs to his left blew up. It was right there, a geyser of water, and it was gone. The Japs destroyed or disabled 72 of the 125 amtracs that were launched during the first three waves. Suddenly a large shell exploded with a terrific concussion, and a huge geyser rose up just to the right front of the little tractor. The engine stalled. They sat stalled, floating in the water for some terrifying moments. They were sitting ducks. The driver was wrestling frantically with the controls and finally got the engine started. They moved forward again, toward the geysers and exploding shells. Thad felt nauseated. He tried to remain calm, telling himself that everything was going to be all right. The shelling would stop. All of the Japanese would be dead. The butterflies in his stomach were out of control; his bladder was about to turn loose.

The bombardment seemed to lift off the beach and move inland. The dive bombers and fighters also moved inland with their bombing and strafing. The Japanese increased the volume of their fire against the waves of amtracs.

"Stand by!" someone yelled.

Thad slung his two medical pouches over his shoulders and buckled his helmet chin strap. Machine gun fire, tracers seemed to come at the marines at eye level. Some piled over the sides of the amtrac; others ran down the ramps. At least they made it all the way to the beach, not like that last fiasco. Thad stepped onto the sand and immediately fell, being pushed by a marine behind him. His only thought was to get up and get off the beach. Machine gun fire slapped the sand all around him. That, along with rifle fire, seemed to be getting heavier. A nearby landing craft exploded, filling the air with black smoke and debris. Amtracs seemed to be burning everywhere, some on the reef, others on the beach.

Thad had never felt so helpless or frightened in his life. He finally managed to get up, and crouching low, reached the inland edge of the sand, seemingly out of the heavy fire hitting the beach. Somehow most of the squad seemed to be together. Gunny Mancillas signaled for them to move to the right and join up with the rest of the company. Soon, they began to move off the beach, with more marines coming in behind them. Officers and NCOs shouted orders amid the confusion.

As soon as they started to move inland, a machine gun opened up from a thicket to their right. Then mortars. Thad fell into a crater. The company was pinned down. He shook. He sweated. He prayed. Hadn't he done this once before? Déjà vu? He survived Tarawa. Now had serious doubts about surviving this stinking island, whatever it was called, fearful that a mortar round would fall directly into his hole. He felt complete helplessness.

The shelling finally lifted, and orders came to move out. Thad got up, covered with coral dust and sand, and on rubbery legs followed the order. He moved out. The walking wounded passed, going the opposite direction, making their way to the beach for evacuation.

As they moved through the thick scrub brush, possibly concealing a regiment of snipers, they got orders to halt in an open area. It was here that Thad came upon his first enemy dead. They appeared to be two riflemen and a corpsman. The corpsman's medical pouch was open with the usual bandages and medicines, and he was lying on his back, his stomach open and exposed. He was probably in the act of treating one or both of the riflemen laying next to him. Thad's thinking was, *Now ain't this something. The first dead Jap I see is a corpsman, or whatever they call themselves, just like me. We got some sort of fate working here? An omen?* As he shook that thought from his mind, Rat began stripping the dead men of souvenirs. He was joined by Willis and three others. Eye glasses, a small Japanese flag, a pistol, identification cards. Rat said he's going to get him one of them big swords. Send it home.

Mortars had begun in the scrub brush and were now walking their way quickly toward their open area. Again they ran away, away from the damn mortar rounds now landing and exploding dangerously close. As they reached more thick scrub, the mortar shelling stopped. Thad looked back in the direction from which they had come, and Watson was down. He wasn't yelling, he was just down. Thad ran back to him.

Watson, one of the new replacements, had been hit in the lung. He gurgled. "I'm sorry, Doc."

Thad listened to his gurgling. "Roll onto the side that hurts."

Watson tried and screamed. Something about Jesus.

"Watson, shut up." He removed Watson's poncho and rolled him over on it.

He screamed again.

"Shut up, or I'll leave you here."

"It hurts."

"It's supposed to hurt."

The hole gurgled like a stopped-up drain. Thad put a dressing over the hole and pulled the dressing tight. Watson was by now too exhausted to scream anymore. "Ohhh. It hurts too much."

"Don't be such a fucking baby, Watson. You wanna die? Lie on it. You tough, Watson? Just hold on. You're going to be okay."

Stretcher bearers carried a marine back towards the beach. The marine, obviously dead, seemed to be in separate parts, a bloody half of a leg was lying on the marine's chest. The other leg was gone. *Couldn't find it I guess.* Thad stopped them, told them, "Leave this guy here, and take this one. He's hurt bad, but he'll make it if you get him out of here. You can come back and get this one."

The two stretcher bearers gently removed what was left of the dead marine and laid him on the ground. Thad thought, *That's good. They could have just dumped the poor guy off.* They placed Watson on the stretcher, and Thad took his hand and told him that he'd see him back in the States. Watson nodded.

Watson and most of the other replacements, new guys, Garza, Banta, Lilly, Pytel, and one named Edward Arnold (Plowboy, naturally), were avoided by the veterans of Betio if at all possible.

They would much rather share a foxhole with someone that knew what the hell he was doing. Thad felt that they were being unfair, but what did he know? He was just a Navy doc. If they were wounded should he treat them any differently? No way.

They moved inland, passing the airfield with shells still passing overhead, headed in both directions. The scrub was slowing them down, but it was offering at least some concealment from the enemy fire. They paused briefly on a north south trail, then continued on, receiving some sniper fire, and soon reached a clearing and were overlooking the ocean, having crossed the southern tip of the island had reached the eastern shore. Rat said, "Are we done, Gunny? We done swept across the whole friggin' island. Can we go home now?"

Word was passed that their Battalion Executive Officer had been killed a few moments after hitting the beach, and that the amtrac carrying most of the battalion's field telephone and radio equipment and operators had been destroyed on the reef. Control and communications was going to be a bitch.

The weather was getting hotter, and Thad was soaked with sweat. He began passing out salt tablets, took a few himself, and took a drink from his canteen. They had been warned to take it easy on the water because no one knew when they would get any more.

A sweating runner came up from the rear. It was the Mouse. Roy Boy said, "Hey, Mouse. How's it hanging, man? These guys are all about your size. You sure you ain't related?"

Mouse gave him the finger, found Captain Bartholomew, and told him, "Battalion CP said that we gotta establish contact with the Seventh Marines, because if the Japs counterattack, they'll come right through the gap between them and us."

The platoons formed up and took casualty reports. Japanese mortar and artillery fire increased, possibly preparing for a counter attack. They moved a short distance to the edge of the scrub. It was late in the afternoon, and Thad looked out over the airfield toward a ridge and saw vehicles moving, kicking up dust. They were enemy tanks.

Shell bursts began appearing among the Jap tanks. Sherman tanks had made it to the edge of the airfield and were delivering the fire. "Get some tanks!"

Word came again to move out. Marines formed a line at the edge of the scrub along a trail, and lay prone, trying to take whatever cover they could. It was all but impossible to dig into the hard coral rock, so the men piled rocks around them whenever they could or got behind fallen trees.

Then the order came, "Stand by to repel counterattack."

Thad figured, *Swell. Just what we need.* It seemed to him that they were alone, and confusion was the order of the day in the middle of utter chaos, with snipers everywhere and no contact with any other units.

Just then a Marine tank to their rear appeared, and for a moment it looked like it was going to open fire on the good guys. Then a Japanese field gun opened up on the tank, the tank swung around, lined up on the gun, and that duel lasted less than a minute. Marine tank, one. Japanese gun, zero. Then, as Thad watched, feeling completely exposed and helpless, the Marine tank swung back around and was taking aim at them. Before the tanker could open fire, a marine jumped up on the tank, trying to get the hatch open, and was shot and killed by a Jap sniper. The tank moved on.

The heavy firing lifted, and the Japanese counterattack had been broken, at least for the time being.

There had been much talk about the Japanese and their "banzai" or suicide attacks. They'd charge into the enemy screaming, "Banzai!" killing as many as they possibly could before they themselves were killed. This last attack was not of the banzai variety, but a well-coordinated tank-infantry attack. Approximately one company of Japanese infantry and about thirteen tanks had moved carefully across the airfield until annihilated by the marines.

At nightfall, the situation was becoming precarious. Charlie Company and the rest of the battalion were isolated, nearly out of water, and ammunition was low. The battalion runner came and directed them into the division's line at the airfield.

As they dug in, Thad's thirst was almost unbearable, his stomach was tied in knots, and he was soaked in sweat. He dissolved some K-ration dextrose in his mouth, and that helped. He took the last sip of water from his canteen, having no idea when relief would get through with additional water. All the while, artillery shells shrieked and whistled back and forth overhead with increasing frequency, and small-arms fire rattled everywhere. An eerie green light of star shells was on their parachutes.

Thad began taking off his boots.

"Doc, what the hell are you doing?" Boudreau, who had rejoined the company at Camp Tarawa, asked.

"Taking off my boondockers. My feet hurt."

"Are you nuts? What the hell are you gonna do in your stocking feet if the Japs come bustin' through that jungle or across the field? We may have to get out of this hole and haul ass. They'll probably pull one of them damn banzai attacks before daybreak, and you're going to be running across this coral without no boots on."

"Okay, okay. I wasn't thinking." I began pulling his boots back on.

Boudreau said, "We'll be lucky to get our boots off before we leave this crummy island."

They settled in for the long night that was surely to follow. Shelling. All night long there were explosions. Shelling. *Maybe they'll run out of ammunition and the shelling will stop. Don't count on it.* Thad had to fight back the almost irresistible urge to scream, to cry. He felt that if this battle, this war, dragged on, he would lose his mind, go completely fucking nuts and be a raving lunatic, a jibbering idiot. Lou Ann would have to nurse him, clothe him, feed him, if she would even have him.

As the night wore on he was barely able to catch even so much as a catnap. Towards dawn, artillery fire was concentrated on the area of scrub that they had vacated earlier in the day. Roy Boy said, "They must think we're still out there. I'll bet when they get it leveled the next counterattack will come from there." The barrage increased in intensity as the Japanese gave the vacant scrub a real pounding.

When the barrage finely subsided, it was Rat that said, "Don't quit now, you bastards. Use up all your damn shells in the wrong place."

Thad and the rest of the battalion weren't aware of the problems on the beach. The problems that they were having in getting supplies unloaded, even if they got as far as the beach. Meanwhile, they hoped and prayed that the water would soon get to them. Empty canteens were the norm.

Still, before dawn, after the artillery shelling had stopped, came the machine-gun fire, intense machine-gun fire, with tracers no more than a foot over their heads. It slowed; Thad thought that it would stop. Then another machine gun opened up, coming from somewhere near the airfield. More tracers, bluish white. American tracers were red. *They got us in a crossfire. Swell.* They stayed low. Tried to get lower. After about fifteen minutes the firing stopped just as suddenly as it had begun, and the cries for corpsman began.

From nearby, someone was saying, "Doc! Help me, Doc!" It was Garza, one of the new guys, from Brownsville. Couldn't be over eighteen years old. Born in Guadalajara, came to Texas with his parents when he was a baby, as they scratched out a living picking vegetables with baby Sergio strapped to his mother's back, moving as the seasons dictated. When Thad reached him, Garza was sitting up, had removed his pack and dungaree jacket, and was holding his arm. He looked as if a round had gone through his upper arm, in and out. Not much more than a flesh wound, but was bleeding heavily. Thad applied a tourniquet, sprinkled sulfa into the open wound, and bandaged it. Several yards away a corpsman was busy treating the wounds of another marine, and shouted to Thad that he needed help. He told Garza to unloosen the tourniquet in a few minutes, and if it was still bleeding do it again. He'd be right back.

The other corpsman told Thad that he could handle this one, but there was another man that needed attention further down to the right. When Thad reached the marine he was barely conscious. He had a stomach wound, a jagged tear, probably a piece of coral or possibly a piece of shrapnel. He once again sprinkled the wound with sulfa, applied a pressure bandage, shot him up with morphine, and could do nothing else for the guy. The man never lost consciousness. Thad told him that he would find stretcher bearers and get him out of there.

He returned to where he had left Garza. He was sitting up, putting on his dungaree jacket. He told Thad he was okay, that the company had moved out, and that they had better get their asses in gear, which is exactly what they did, all the while Thad looking for a stretcher to send back to the man with the stomach wound.

13

Dawn finally came, and along with it, an unbearable thirst. "Where the hells our water? We ain't going to make it unless we get some water up here, pronto." The company had already suffered many cases of heat prostration.

Someone called, "Come on. We've found a well." Men gathered at a hole about ten feet deep. At the bottom was a small pool of milky-looking water. One of the men in the hole was filling canteens and passing them up. The men drank, never mind the taste.

Thad, torn between thirst and his duty as a corpsman, told them not to drink the water. "It's got to be contaminated. You'll probably get dysentery if you're lucky enough to live."

Sure enough, those who had drank the water soon began throwing up. Diarrhea and dysentery to come later.

The order came. "Stand by to move out." It was then that a detail came up with water cans, ammunition and rations.

"Thank you, Lord."

They poured water out of five gallon cans into canteen cups. The water looked brown. It had a blue film of oil floating on the surface. It tasted awful. Then came the cramps. The oil drums had been emptied of the oil, then cleaned and filled with water. Obviously they had not been cleaned well enough. As awful as the stuff was it was either drink it or suffer heat exhaustion, so they drank.

Gear was gathered, and they prepared to move out in preparation for the attack across the airfield. The Japanese shelling had begun at daylight. They scrambled to get into position for the attack and were told to hold until they were told to move again. The Japanese shelling was getting heavier. Artillery fire was being laid down across the airfield in preparation for the attack. Thad knew that when the shelling stopped they would move.

Lieutenant Pond stood up, said, "Let's go."

They moved at a walk, then a trot. Several battalions of marines moved across the airfield. A high ridge, Umurbrogol Ridge, to become known as Bloody Nose Ridge, towards the end of the airfield gave the enemy a decided advantage. They could deliver mortar fire, artillery fire, rifle fire, or any damn kind of fire they wanted on the exposed marines, and they did. Thad thought, *Perfect. All we need now while we're hauling ass across the damn airfield is to be strafed by a squadron of Zero's.*

As they ran, an NCO hurried by yelling, "Keep moving, you guys. There's less chance that you'll be hit if you go across fast, and don't stop."

Really?

Four Marine infantry battalions moved out, completely dominated by the fire from Bloody Nose Ridge. They moved rapidly in the open through ever-increasing enemy fire. The shells screeched and whistled, exploding all around them. They were completely exposed, running through a shower of deadly metal and the constant crash of explosions. *Yea, though I walk through the valley of the shadow of death, I will fear no evil, for Thou art with me.*

It was hot, unbearably hot, and the heat was exhausting. Smoke and dust from the barrage limited their vision. The ground shook under the concussions. Japanese bullets snapped and cracked all around and seemed almost insignificant compared with the erupting shells. Chunks of coral stung Thad's hands and face.

The further they went the worse it got. Marines were stumbling and falling as they got hit. They passed several craters that would afford at least some degree of cover, but were ordered to keep moving. Because of the superb discipline and leadership, it never occurred to the marines that the attack might fail. Thad, however, had his doubts.

About halfway across Thad stumbled and fell as a shell exploded to his left. On his right, Boudreau let out a grunt as a piece of shrapnel struck him. Thad ran to him and found that the shrapnel had struck him in his pack, ripping a hole in it and not Boudreau. He was smiling, still smiling. Thad couldn't believe it. He said, "*Je suis d'accord, mon cher.* I'm okay. Just knocked the wind out of me."

Thad picked up the piece of shrapnel that probably had struck Boudreau. It was still hot. He showed it to him and stuck it in his pack. "C'mon. Get up. We gotta get out of here."

After what seemed like a day and a half, they finally made it across the airfield to the somewhat limited protection of low bushes. "Maybe if they can't see us, they can't hit us. Maybe if a frog had wings…"

The heat was intolerable. The temperature that day was 105 degrees, and it would get hotter. Thad tagged several marines with heat prostration as being too weak to continue. They were evacuated. Because the island was so small it was always a short carry to the beach. Thad's boondockers were literally filled with sweat. When he would lie on his back and hold up his legs, water would drip out of them. Walking on water? Don't even think about it.

The company moved out through a swampy area and dug in for the night. The sniper fire hadn't been as intense as before. Thad spent most of the night treating the wounded. One marine had a bullet hole through his upper chest. The round went through his dog tags and missed his St. Christopher medal. "Protect us, St. Christopher." Marines went back out on the airfield, under the cover of darkness, and brought in wounded and dead. Thad attended to all that he could, his two medical pouches running dangerously low on medicines, bandages, sulfa, morphine, and especially salt tablets. He would have to get back to the beach to the aid station and get his pouches refitted unless he could find the Mouse and get him to do it for him.

He found the little runner, and Mouse told him that he had to go back to the beach to get whatever communication equipment he could scrounge up and would have too much to carry, if there was any equipment available. Thad would have to go with him.

On the way, the Mouse told him that he didn't like being called Shit House Mouse. He didn't appreciate being called Runt, Shorty, Short Round, Half Pint, Feather Merchant, or any of the other handles that had been hung on him. His name was Raymond, by God, that's what his mother named him, and he would like for everyone to call him by name, Raymond, and would Thad pass the word around. Thad told him that no one was being disrespectful. Most everyone had a nickname, but he would try.

When they reached the beach, Thad went to find the aid station while the Mouse, Raymond, went off in search communications gear. He found the aid station, and rather than getting replacement items, he picked up two brand new pouches already filled, leaving his, half empty.

Raymond, the Mouse, found Thad. The little guy was loaded down with a PRC 10 radio, two walkie talkies, a field telephone, and a roll of communications wire. Luckily he had left his pack back on the line or he would have never been able to carry it all. Thad grabbed the roll of wire, and they trudged back to the company. Thad and Raymond had not been able to locate the water detail, and they were still short of water. Everyone was weakened by the heat, physically and mentally exhausted, and the second night had just begun.

The enemy infiltration that followed was intense. Illumination lit the sky above the airfield, and the Japanese began to infiltrate all along the company front as well as their rear along the shore. *Swell. We're surrounded.* Sporadic bursts of small-arms fire, while the marines maintained fire discipline. Thad was dug in behind a small pile of coral, along with the Gunny and Rat. There was movement in the dried brush in front of them. Gunny and Rat aimed their M-1s in the direction of the noise, and Thad stayed back, his .45 cocked and unlocked, expecting at any second for a wild-eyed Jap to come running out of the brush, shooting and shouting, "Banzai!" It didn't happen. His heart rate returned to normal. Then more rustling, then silence. Then again, rustling, then silence. It must be a Jap trying to slip in as close as possible. Thad wanted to empty his pistol into the brush. Gunny told him to relax.

"Oh, yeah. Fire discipline." Finally, a helmeted figure stood up, and asked the little group if they had any water. It was a marine. Gunny called him a stupid son of a bitch, told him he came this close to getting killed and to get out of his sight. Poor guy, maybe delusional. He wouldn't be the first or last.

Thad put his .45 back on safe and returned it to its holster. He leaned against the coral and waited. Waited for what? The dawn? The Japs to overrun them? Get up and move out again? It was the latter. "Get your gear on, and stand by to move out."

They began moving slowly out of the thick swamp. As Thad passed one shallow foxhole where Fredrickson had been dug in, he asked a man nearby if it was true that Booger Red had been killed. Sadly he said yes. He had been fatally wounded in the head. Booger Red was a bright young man who aspired to be a fireman, who'd save lives rather than take them. *What a waste*, he thought. *Organized madness that destroys the nation's best.* It made him wonder about the hopes and aspirations of a dead Japanese lying near Booger Red.

They continued to move out, keeping a five-pace interval through the thick swamp toward the sound of heavy firing. The heat was unbearable, and they were halted frequently to prevent heat prostration.

They had made it to the eastern edge of the airfield and halted in the shade of a scrub thicket. They fell on the deck sweating, panting, exhausted. Thad reached for his canteen when a rifle bullet snapped overhead.

"He's close. Get down!" said Sergeant Bradley. The rifle cracked again. "Sounds like he's right through there," pointing at thick brush no more than thirty yards away.

"I'll go get him," said Rat.

"Okay, go ahead, but watch yourself."

Rat grabbed his rifle and took off into the scrub with the nonchalance of a hunter going after a rabbit in a bush. Not bad for a city boy, especially a New York City boy. The Blind Ducks would be proud. He angled to one side so as to steal up on the sniper from the rear. After two M-1 shots a grinning Rat reappeared, carrying a Japanese rifle and some personal effects.

They later moved out through some knee-high bushes into an open area at the edge of the airfield. They continued on until Bloody Nose Ridge was on their left. They started receiving heavy fire. The Japanese observers on the ridge had a clear, unobstructed view of the marines and could deliver fire whenever and wherever they wanted. Thad and the boys of Charlie Company were pinned down, having their first taste of Bloody Nose Ridge.

Whenever a small group of men tried to move, Japanese mortars opened up on them. If the whole company tried to move here came the artillery. The Japanese were demonstrating excellent fire discipline, firing only when they could inflict maximum casualties, and their firing positions on the ridge were well camouflaged, making it impossible for the planes to destroy them. They were firing from caves, and when they ceased fire, they would shut steel doors and wait while artillery and naval guns blasted away at the rock. When that firing stopped they'd open the doors and go at it again.

Ammunition, K rations, and water had been delivered by an amtrac before dark. The marines, before settling in for the night, dug into the rations. Darkness obscured them from Japanese observers, but the artillery harassing fire continued.

Early the next morning, artillery and mortars shelled known Japanese positions to their front and the marines continued their attack along the left side of Bloody Nose Ridge. Shelling from the ridge positions slowed them down. Planes made air strikes, ships and artillery attacked the ridges, but Japanese shells kept coming in. The number of casualties was increasing, and the attack was finally called off about noon.

Thad figured, *I ain't no military strategist, but it seems to me that whoever controls that ridge, controls the whole damn island.*

Aerial photos showed Umurbrogol Ridge as a rather gently rounded north-south hill. Instead of a gently rounded hill, the Ridge was, in fact, a complex system of sharply uplifted coral ridges, knobs, valleys, and sink holes. It rose above the remainder of the island anywhere from fifty to three hundred feet and provided excellent emplacements for cave and tunnel defenses. The Japanese made the most of it.

14

The following day Charlie Company received an order to push a strong combat patrol to the east coast of the island. Their orders were to move onto the peninsula that formed the smaller "claw" of the lobster, and set up a defensive position.

Lieutenant Pond commanded this little patrol, which consisted of about forty marines plus a war dog, a Doberman pinscher that could locate enemy unseen by the marines. They were heavily armed with rifles and BARs, plus a couple of machine gun squads and a mortar squad. It was reported that a couple of thousand Japs were somewhere on the other side of an adjacent swamp.

They picked up rations and extra ammunition as they headed into the thick scrub brush. Leaving the battalion, Thad felt the company was like a little boy leaving home for the first time. The company had become his family, and he belonged there. Boudreau, Rat, Joe Louis Boyd, and all the rest had become his brothers. He lived with them, treated them, fought with them, laughed with them, sometimes cried with them, and might die with them. This time, this place, he belonged here.

They moved through the brush quietly in a strung-out

formation with scouts out front looking for Jap snipers. Things were quiet, but not so on the ridge. They continued through a swamp choked with mangroves with its tangle of roots, which made walking with a heavy load difficult. They stopped at an abandoned Japanese machine gun bunker made of coconut logs and coral rock. The bunker would serve as the platoon CP (Command Post). They deployed and dug in around it. The area was just a few feet above water level. They maintained silence, aimed their weapons to where they would more than likely fire, and settled in for a long night.

They received the password as darkness fell, and a drizzling rain began. It was the darkest night that Thad had ever seen. He could barely see Willis, who was only a few feet away. They were stuck out here in the middle of a damn swamp, and he began to feel as if they were expendable. He had been taught to value life, and to find yourself in a situation where your life is of little value is a humbling experience.

The hours dragged on. In the dripping darkness they strained their eyes and ears for any sign of enemy movement. From somewhere near the CP, a voice sounded: "Help me! Oh, God, help me!" He became louder and began thrashing around.

"Someone better shut him up before every Jap in this damn swamp knows our position." The poor marine had cracked up. The stress of combat had become too much.

Sergeant Bradley held the man's arms to his side tried to calm the man down, trying to reassure him that he was going to be all right. He just got louder. The sergeant sent for the doc, and when Thad got there, the marine was struggling and screaming at the top of his voice. Someone slugged him in the jaw in an attempt to knock him out. Didn't work. Thad gave him an injection of morphine hoping that would calm him down. It didn't . Another hit of morphine. It had no effect either. Finally there was the sickening thud of an entrenching tool crashing into the man's head, and he was finally silenced.

A little after daylight, Thad went back to the CP to check on the marine. He was dead. The others in the CP had done what had to be done.

Lieutenant Pond radioed battalion telling them that he wanted to bring the patrol in. He was told to stay put for a couple of days until the disposition of the Japanese could be determined. The lieutenant calmly disagreed, saying they hadn't fired a shot and because of the circumstances they all had a pretty bad case of nerves.

The battalion CO finally agreed, and told the lieutenant that he would send a relief column and a tank so they wouldn't have any trouble coming in. The word was passed, and everyone breathed easier. The relief column and the tank finally arrived, and they placed the body on the tank and returned to the company. Thad never heard a word about the marine's death.

On the tenth day of the battle (D +10), Chesty Puller's First Marine Regiment, nearly wiped out, was relieved by the U.S. Army's 321st Infantry Regiment. When the First Marines formed up, companies looked like platoons. Platoons looked like squads. Some companies had only twenty men remaining.

The men of Charlie Company boarded trucks that carried them past the airfield. They were amazed at the work already accomplished on the airfield by the Seabees. Heavy construction equipment was everywhere. They were making progress and seemed unfazed by the war going on all around them.

They continued on parallel to Bloody Nose Ridge, and were fired on by small arms, artillery, and mortars from the high ridges. At dusk they climbed down from the trucks and settled in for the night.

Later Thad shared a foxhole with Willis. Both were awake. It would soon be time for their turn to be on watch. Willis was turning out to be all right. He had shed most of his excess weight, and while he wasn't exactly a hard charger, he was doing his share of the fighting. They had learned that Willis' dream was to get into politics. Therefore he was "Governor." He had briefly attended some little school in Delaware, studying Political Science. When the war was over, if ever, he was going back to school, get his degree, and return to Dover and try to get elected to the city council and go on from there. Maybe to Wilmington, get involved in the state government and after that, who knows? Thad figured he had his sights set on Washington, but never came out and said it. "That's okay. You gotta have a dream." Thad's dream was to get off this island in one piece.

"What do you think, Governor? We gonna' have a quiet night?"

"We haven't had one so far. Why should tonight be any different?"

"I don't know. Sure would be nice, though."

Just then two figures sprang up from a shallow ditch directly across the road from them. Arms waving, screaming, babbling in Japanese, here they came. Thad had his .45 out, wishing he still had the carbine. He aimed at one of the figures that had moved to his right as he disappeared into a foxhole, and Thad and the Governor turned to see the other just as he jumped in their foxhole, waving his bayonet, screaming wildly. He landed on top of Thad, pinning him to the ground. In the cramped little foxhole the Governor couldn't even get his M-1 in position to fire, so he had grabbed it by the barrel, stood up, raised like it was a sledge hammer, and brought it down on the helmet of Jap. Thad heard the "thunk," felt the Jap relax enough for him to free his hand with his .45, and he put a round into the Jap's side. He grunted, and ended up face to face with Thad, like some sort of romantic embrace. He freed himself and put another round into back of the Jap's head. He looked for Willis, who was running toward the foxhole where the first Jap had disappeared. Once again, the Governor had his rifle by the barrel and appeared to be beating the crap out something or someone. He looked like he was chopping wood or trying to ring the bell at the county fair. When Thad reached him the Jap was either dead, not far from it, or maybe he wished he was dead. The Jap didn't have the benefit of a helmet. His head and face was no more than a bloody mass of bone and flesh. The stock of Governor's rifle was split.

He was breathing heavily. He saw Thad, and said, "Kill him, Doc." Thad knew that this guy was not going to get any deader than he already was, but fired a shot into what was left of the Jap's face anyhow.

"I think I broke my rifle, Doc."

"Don't worry about it, Gov. We'll get you another one. You done good."

The next morning they got word that the battalion would be moving north to Ngesebus Island. The Japs had been moving in reinforcements by barge down to Peleliu from the larger islands to the north. While some of the barges had been destroyed, several hundred Japanese troops had made it ashore. The battalion had been ordered to hit the beach on Ngesebus Island tomorrow.

The battalion moved into an area near the northern peninsula and dug in for the night. The troops didn't know what to expect on Ngesebus. Thad prayed that it wouldn't be a repeat of the horrors of D-Day.

Early the next morning they stood by to board the amtracs that would take them the five hundred yards across the shallow reef to the beach, while ships fired on the island, followed by strafing and bombing by Marine F4U Corsairs. Someone said, "We're going to have lots of support on this one."

Roy Boy replied, "Don't count on it."

The amtracs moved to the water's edge and waited as the naval bombardment covered the little island with smoke and dust. The Corsairs plastered the beach with machine-gun fire, bombs, and rockets, while the marines cheered, yelled, and waved at the pilots who would wait until the very last instant before pulling out of their dives.

At H hour tractor drivers revved up their engines and moved out into the water and started the assault. Thad's heart was pounding, and he wondered if his luck would hold out. This was his third landing, and as far as he was concerned, practice don't make perfect.

Much to his relief they didn't receive fire as they approached the island. When the amtrac lurched to a stop well up on the beach, the tailgate dropped, and the marines scrambled out, while the bombardment continued well to their front.

Thad, along with Rat, Boudreau, and Pytel and Banta, two of the new guys, moved inland a short distance, but when they got to the edge of the airstrip a Japanese machine gun opened up on them.

They huddled behind a coral rock as the machine gun slugs zipped overhead. Because the rock was small, they were huddled together shoulder to shoulder, when Banta, to Thad's right, screamed, "I'm hit!" He grabbed his left elbow with his right hand, groaning with pain as he thrashed around.

Thad cut away the sleeve of the bloody dungaree jacket with his K-BAR, while Pytel with his K-BAR worked to remove the injured marine's pack. He placed the razor-sharp knife under the thick web pack strap, gave a jerk, and ended up cutting Thad in the face, a deep cut running from below his left ear to the middle of his cheek. He recoiled in pain as blood flowed down his face, returned to the work at hand, and told Boudreau to get a pressure bandage out of his pouch and hold it to his face while he worked on the injured arm. He managed to stop the bleeding, dressed the wound and had the injured man place his arm into the front of his dungaree jacket. With nothing to fashion a sling out of it was the best he could do.

When the machine gun was finally silenced, Thad took the wounded man back to the beach where a temporary aid station had been set up and had his own wound tended to. A doctor stitched up the nasty gash, bandaged it, and Thad was back with the company in a matter of a few hours.

During his absence, Rat managed to deliver a solid right to the mouth of Pytel. Nothing said, just a wicked right hand that put Pytel down for the count. When Thad returned and asked him what happened to Pytel's mouth, Rat told him a piece of coral must have kicked up from one of the machine gun rounds. Thad said, "Oh," and delivered a roundhouse right of his own, catching Pytel flush on the jaw, and he went down again.

Rat leaned over and asked him, "Think you'll learn to be more careful?"

Pytel nodded in the affirmative.

"Please try."

In the days that followed, Thad washed his wound with water from his canteen, applied sulfa powder, and had Boudreau change the dressing. Boudreau even offered to remove the stitches, but Thad said, "I don't think so."

"Do I get a Purple Heart for this?"

"I don't think so."

Meanwhile, the silenced machine gun nest that had been quieted was no longer quiet, but this time the marines were in a more advantageous position and could possibly take the damn thing out. The bunker was concrete, covered with a couple feet of sand, with four gun ports about twelve inches wide by six inches, and two vents sticking out the top, doors on each end.

By now they had been joined by others from the platoon, including the Gunny and Sergeant Bradley. Bradley told Boudreau to go around the side and see if he could shove a grenade through one of the ports. The Cajun said, "Consider it done, *Monsieur* Gunny." he made it around to the side, jammed a grenade through the gun port, and damned if the Japs didn't toss it right back out. This happened two more times. Boudreau would pull the pin, let the spoon go, and hold on to the grenade as long as he felt was safe and then shove it through the opening, but the Japs were quick. Sergeant Bradley finally joined Boudreau, climbed up on top of the bunker and dropped two grenades down each of the vents, and those, too, those were pitched out. The sergeant finally lay down and stuck his carbine through one of the ports and emptied a full magazine.

The machine gun was obviously still fully operational. While they took cover Rat was sent to find a flame thrower. When he returned with the flame thrower, he was followed by one of the amtracs. Thad was thinking, *Gotcha. Ain't gonna' be no more of this shove-grenade-in, toss-grenade-out nonsense.*

The Japanese inside the bunker, seeing all this, realized the game is over, and started coming out. Running, shooting, they were cut down by the riflemen not long after they cleared the doors. The gunner on the amtrac fired three armor-piercing 75 mm shells at close range. The third round tore a hole through the side of the pillbox, the flame thrower aimed the nozzle at the opening made by the gun, pressed the trigger, *whoosh*, and all was quiet inside. The pillbox was out of action thanks to the flame thrower and the amtrac.

The next morning, with the help of tanks and amtracs, Ngesebus was secured, and they were to be relieved by an Army unit. The marines had suffered fifteen killed and thirty-three wounded. The Japanese lost 470 killed and thirty-four wounded.

The stress of continuous battle was beginning to show on the marines. They would sit, looking at nothing: the thousand-yard stare, a hollow-eyed, vacant look. The shock, horror, fear, and fatigue of fifteen days of combat was wearing them down physically and emotionally.

"Three days, maybe four," the Division C.O. had said before Peleliu. Now they had been at it for fifteen terrible days with no end in sight.

Thad felt himself choking up. He turned his back on the rest of the company, sat on his helmet, put his head in his hands and tried to shut out reality. He cried. The more he tried to stop, the worse it got. He sobbed. His body shook. He was sickened and revolted, having seen so many young men maimed and killed day after day. He was tired, wrung out emotionally, and he felt he couldn't take it any more. He had no idea that he was only halfway through with this month-long ordeal.

He felt a hand on his shoulder. It was Lieutenant Pond. He said, "What's the matter, Doc?" Thad told him how he felt, and the Lieutenant said, "I know what you mean. I feel the same way. But we gotta keep going. It will be over soon, and we'll be off of this God-forsaken island." His understanding gave Thad the strength he needed, strength to endure fifteen more terrible days and nights.

Long lines of soldiers came by accompanied by amtracs loaded with supplies, and they received orders to move out. They walked wearily toward the beach. They crossed back to northern Peleliu where they settled in east of Umurbrogel Mountain, where they had been during the first week of the campaign. It was fairly quiet, and they were able to rest, but it was an uneasy rest.

15

They were given the order to draw rations and ammunition. The battalion was going to reinforce the marines on Bloody Nose Ridge. By now, the losses on the ridges had become critical, but all of Peleliu, with the exception of the Bloody Nose Ridge, was in Marine hands. The enemy held on to an area about four hundred yards by twelve hundred yards in the most rugged, worst part of the ridges, the Umurbrogol Pocket. The terrain was unbelievably rugged, jumbled, and confusing.

Thad was resigned to the dismal conclusion that he wasn't going to leave the island until all the Japs were dead, or he was hit, and getting wounded seemed inevitable. It was just a matter of time. One couldn't hope to continue to avoid the law of averages forever, but he couldn't quite visualize his own death. He merely existed hour to hour, from day to day, treating, bandaging, offering words of encouragement to boys who had become men just days, weeks, or months before. Numbed by fear and fatigue, he didn't have the option of being concerned with only his survival. The survival of others was his responsibility and was not taken lightly. He had taken an oath, which was never far from his mind. He determined that as long as he was physically able he would continue treating, bandaging, and offering words of encouragement. Words of encouragement to those who knew they were drawing their last breaths. Why?

On 3 October the battalion made an attack on the Five Sisters, a rugged coral hill with five nearly vertical peaks. Before the attack the Eleventh Marines shelled the area with an artillery barrage, and the machine guns laid down a covering fire.

Riflemen moved forward into the slopes before Japanese fire stopped them. They pulled back and the same fruitless attack was repeated the next day with he same dismal result.

Stretcher bearers rushed into the fray picking up wounded under fire, and returning them to relative safety behind coral outcroppings where they would be treated by Thad and other corpsmen. For the Japanese, the stretcher bearers were fair game, and several were killed.

Thad marveled at the attitude of the casualties. When conscious, the wounded marine seemed at ease and supremely confident that they would get him out alive, while Thad doubted that any of them, himself included, would make it. The not-so-seriously-hurt were usually in high spirits and relieved. They were on their way out of hell, and they expressed pity for those left behind. The more seriously wounded and the dying were carried to an amtrac or ambulance jeep that rushed them to the battalion aid station.

By now the entire company was in open ground, the Japanese watching from the Five Sisters. They came under fire only when the Japs were sure of inflicting maximum casualties. Their fire discipline was superb, and when they fired someone usually got hit.

When night came the enemy came out of their caves, infiltrating and creeping up on the marine's lines to raid all night, every night. Raids by individual soldiers or small groups began as soon as darkness fell. Their ability to creep in silently over rough rocks was incredible. They knew the terrain perfectly. They would rush in suddenly, jabbering incoherent sounds, sometimes throwing a grenade, but always swinging a saber, bayonet, or knife.

When daylight came Thad walked a short distance to relieve himself. As he stepped over a log his foot came down squarely on the back of a Jap hiding behind the log. Thad whipped out his .45 and aimed at the chest of the Jap as he jumped to his feet. He pulled the trigger. *Click.* No round in the chamber. The enemy soldier pulled the pin from a grenade, and Thad threw his .45 at him, spun around, ran back toward the company yelling, "Shoot him!" The Japanese threw his grenade, hitting Thad in the back. It fell to the deck and lay there. It was a dud. The Japanese then drew his bayonet, waving it like a sword, and took off after the corpsman at a dead run.

Thad spotted a BARman and ran toward him yelling for him to shoot the guy. The BARman stood up but didn't fire. Thad, running as hard as he could, was yelling with the Jap in hot pursuit. The BARman finally took aim at the enemy soldier and emptied a twenty-round magazine into him, cutting the body nearly in two.

Terrified and winded, Thad asked the BARman why in the hell he waited so long to fire. Grinning, the BARman said the whole thing reminded him of one of those cartoons with the coyote chasing the roadrunner. He said he was waiting for Thad to say, "Beep, Beep!"

He thought about slugging the guy but was too tired, too relieved to still be alive and in one piece. Instead of slugging him, he thanked him.

Relieving himself was no longer a problem, and he received

permission to go back to battalion headquarters to draw a clean pair of trousers. While there he went to the aid station and had his stitches removed. He returned to the company, found his .45 that he had thrown at the Jap, slammed a round into the chamber, and silently cursed himself for being so unforgivably negligent and stupid.

He borrowed the Governor's little metal mirror so he could have a look at his wound. "Not too bad. Didn't that gangster Al Capone have a scar like this?" He made it clear that anyone calling him "Scarface" would be pistol whipped.

By now, the Umurbrogol Ridge was completely surrounded, the remainder of the island being relatively secure. Souvenir hunters would come up from the rear, relieving whatever they could from the dead Japanese soldiers.

During a lull in the fighting (there were lulls, even though there was always firing going on somewhere) two neat, clean, fresh-looking marines, headed toward the Five Sisters passed Thad, Boudreau, and Joe Louis Boyd, who were eating their K rations. The men called back, "Where's the front line?"

"You just passed through it," answered Boudreau.

The two marines looked at each other, at Thad, Boudreau, and Joe Louis Boyd, and took off in the opposite direction.

After attacking the Five Sisters for four days, the battalion was ordered to make an assault up a large draw called the "Horseshoe." There were numerous heavy guns hidden in the caves in the ridges bordering the Horseshoe, and the battalion was to knock out as many of them as possible.

The attack was preceded by heavy artillery fire, and the attack was surprisingly effective. The Horseshoe wasn't secured, but many Japanese were killed.

Shortly thereafter, the battalion pulled back from the ridges, and went up once again toward the northern end of the island, setting up only yards from the beach. One night, Lieutenant Pond, while making his rounds checking on his troops, stopped at the foxhole manned by Thad and Roy Boy. Thad assured him that everything was cool, then, looking toward the beach, asked the lieutenant if he could borrow his carbine for just a minute. He didn't know what Thad had seen, but followed his gaze toward the sea. In the semi-darkness a figure was moving slowly and silently along the reef in the shallow water paralleling the shoreline. The man couldn't have been more than thirty yards away and couldn't have been seen if it wasn't for the moonlight. There was no doubt that the man was a Japanese trying to get ashore and creep up on the company, and Thad knew that he couldn't hit the man with his .45 at that distance.

Thad rested his elbows on his knees and took careful aim. Two quick pops and the Jap disappeared. He flipped the safety back on, handed the carbine back and said, "Thanks, Lieutenant."

"Doc, we're going to make a marine out of you yet."

During the morning of 15 October, soldiers of the Eighty-First Infantry Division began moving single file into the battalion area. They were being relieved, and soon they were on their way back to the northern end of the island. They camped on a sandy flat area near the beach. They had good rations and enjoyed being out of the line where they could relax. Good water was brought up by jeep. Teeth were brushed, faces and hair washed. They were ordered to shave. They drew clean dungarees, and rumors began to spread that they would soon board ship and leave Peleliu.

On 30 October they squared away their packs and moved out to board ship. They were leaving bloody Peleliu at last.

The cost in casualties for a tiny island was terrible, forty-five days of terrible. The First Marine Division was shattered. It suffered a total loss of 6,526 men: 1,1252 dead, and 5,274 wounded. Most of the enemy garrison on Peleliu died. Only a few were captured. Estimates as to the exact number of losses by the Japanese vary somewhat, but conservatively, 10,900 Japanese soldiers died.

The battle that was planned to take only three days. It took over five months, with the main part of the battle taking about thirty days. The remaining four months were spent finding the remaining Japanese forces hiding out in caves and jungle areas on the northern half of the island. The fact that these guys were not afraid of dying, and they believed it to be dishonorable to be captured, made capturing or even fighting them very difficult.

They boarded a big merchant troopship and had to climb a cargo net to get aboard. They had done this many times during training, but never when they were so exhausted. They had a hard time even getting started. Several stopped to rest on the way up, and the heavy sea didn't help.

Eventually they all made it and were assigned to their quarters. Thad stowed his gear on his rack, and went topside just to breathe the salt air, fresh clean air that wasn't heavy with dust and the stench of death.

There were showers, plenty of fresh, cold water, and hot chow. Life was good, at least for now. Now. The past was over and done with, and they had no control over tomorrow, so they enjoyed it and hoped that the ship didn't stop until it gets to San Diego.

Putting those thoughts aside, the veterans of Peleliu knew that they had accomplished something special. That these marines had been able to survive the intense physical exertion of weeks of combat in the incredible muggy heat gave evidence to their toughness. They had survived emotionally and physically, at least for the time being, thanks to their discipline and training. They were prepared for the worst. On Peleliu, they had faced the worst.

16
Pavavu

Seven days after boarding ship they entered Macquitti Bay and prepared to debark. They had been transported to the island of Pavuvu in the Solomons. Those marines that had trained here prior to the invasion of Peleliu, called it, "A stinking little rat-infested island." Thad didn't care what they called it. It beat the hell out of where they had come from. All the while he was hoping, praying actually, that his next boat ride would deliver him safely back to the states. *Surely they can't expect a man to survive more than two of these invasions of little islands that're costing so many American lives, can they?*

Soon after they debarked, on the beach they found that several tables set up. Behind each table were American Red Cross girls serving grapefruit juice in little paper cups. Some of the men accepted their little paper cups of grapefruit juice mumbling their thanks, some tried to flirt, and others, for some unknown reason, resented the women's being here.

They soon boarded trucks, were driven through the huge tent area, and when they finally arrived at their tent, Thad, Rat,

Boudreau, the Governor, and Joe Louis Boyd noticed the self-conscious replacements. They appeared to be so innocent and unassuming, unaware of what lay ahead, that Thad felt sorry for them.

Shortly after they arrived, with all of the replacements out on work details, Sergeant Bradley ordered the survivors of Peleliu to fall in on the company street. Thad looked around and was surprised at how few remained out of the original 235 men they had started with.

All that the sergeant had to say was that they should be proud. They had fought well in two of the toughest battles the Marine Corps had ever been in, and that they had upheld the honor of the Corps. "You people have proved that you are good marines." He dismissed them.

Their sea bags and cots had been stacked around the center pole of the tents, and when they started unstacking them, the land crabs moved out. Rat started yelling, cursing the crabs while smashing them with his bayonet and entrenching tool while the others cheered him on. "There goes one! One's getting away, Rat. Get him!"

That first week, and the weeks that followed were spent resting, reading, and writing letters, trying to forget the unforgettable. Christmas came, and they feasted on real turkey. Turkey again on New Year's Eve. Thad had decided that Pauvu wasn't so bad after all. It was nothing compared to Camp Tarawa, liberties, girls, but it was a dang sight better than being shot at.

By now they had a new Division Commander, who ordered regular close-order drills, parades, and reviews. It was better than work parties and seemed to help morale. A regular beer ration of two cans a man each week also helped. During close-order drill and parades they dressed in clean khakis, which the men pressed under the mattress pad on their cots.

After they had been on Pavuvu several weeks, Thad was told to dress in clean khakis and report to the company headquarters. He was hoping that someone would tell him, "Good job. You're going home."

When he arrived a company headquarters he was sent to a tent a short distance away, near the battalion headquarters. He reported to the tent and was greeted by a first lieutenant. He asked about Thad's background and education. How did he feel about joining the Navy and ending up as a Marine Corps doc? Thad told him that he was proud, but he had seen enough of the fighting on Tarawa and Peleliu and was ready to go home.

Then the lieutenant got serious and asked him, "How would you feel about sending men into a situation where you knew they would be killed?"

Without hesitation, he answered, "I couldn't do it, sir."

The lieutenant looked at him long and hard and said, "How would you like to be an officer? A transfer from the Navy to the Marine Corps can be arranged with no problem."

If that's the only way I can get back to the states, I'll do it."

The lieutenant laughed and said, "That'll be all."

He returned to the company, knowing full well that he had no desire to leave his friends. The company was home to him, and he had a strong feeling of belonging, no matter how miserable or dangerous conditions might be. He had found his niche as a corpsman and was confident he could do more good as a corpsman than as a second lieutenant. He had no desire to be an officer or to command anybody. He just wanted to be the best corpsman he could be and survive the war. He would turn down the offer if it came. *What the hell's wrong with me?*

During the third month on Pavuvu hepatitis broke out among the troops. Several men in the platoon came down with it, including Thad. The whites of his eyes seemed to yellow, and his skin took on a yellowish appearance. He always felt tired, and the smell of food nauseated him. He went to sick bay, thought he should be hospitalized. Instead was given the Marine Corps remedy for all every illness, the magical APC pill. The All Purpose Capsule was the remedy for everything except bayonet, gunshot, or shrapnel wounds. He was given a light-duty slip, and after several days, was pronounced fit, and training intensified.

During January 1945, the company boarded an LCI (Landing Craft Infantry, a miniature LST) in convoy with other LCI's and went to Guadalcanal for maneuvers.

While aboard the LCI's they listened with interest to daily news reports of the terrible fighting encountered by the Third, Fourth, and Fifth Marine Divisions during the battle for Iwo Jima that began on 19 February. To them it seemed like a larger version of Peleliu, and in most respects, it was. When the island was finally secured on 16 March, the cost to the three Marine Divisions was similar to Peleliu casualties times three.

One day the Governor showed the rest of the platoon a National Geographic map of the Northern Pacific. He pointed out an oddly shaped island just 325 miles south of the southern tip of Japan. It was called Okinawa. Logic told them that Okinawa would be the next stop. If so, the battle was bound to be bitter and bloody. The pattern of the war till then had been the closer they got to Japan, the more vicious the battles became.

During their training they were told they would have to climb over a sea wall or cliff to move inland during the coming battle. Several times, using ropes, they had practiced scaling a sheer coral cliff about forty feet high across the bay from the division's camp on Pavuvu. The general consensus was that if the next landing was anything like the last, they would all be picked off before they even got up any cliff.

They got their required shots and started packing up their gear. They would have more maneuvers on Guadalcanal, then one more time board ships and shove off for their next fight, Okinawa.

17
Guadalcanal

Since the Battle of Guadalcanal, August 1942 to February 1943, the Allied forces' first offensive operation against the Empire of Japan, the island had become a big base, and many service troops and rear-echelon units were stationed there. The name of the island held an important significance to the marines that were to train there in preparation for the invasion of Okinawa.

While they were ashore they strung their jungle hammocks and made themselves as comfortable as possible. Each day for several days they went out into the hills, jungles, and grass fields for training and enjoyed a cool shower each afternoon after coming in from the field.

Since Thad's battalion had been in the assault waves at Peleliu, in the Okinawa campaign they were assigned as regimental reserve. Consequently, for the voyage to the island they would be loaded aboard an attack-transport ship rather than a LST. They would be sent ashore in Higgins boats rather than amphibious tractors. They trained by landing on one of the nearby islands.

One afternoon following landing exercises and field problems, the company returned to the beach to await the return of the Higgins boats that would pick them up and return them to the ship. Dozens of Higgins boats and other amphibious craft motored in from ships to shore, loading marines and ferrying them out to the ships. To Thad it looked like some sort of damned sailing regatta, except that all of the craft were military.

One by one the Higgins boats picked up men, about twenty-five at a time, from their beach area. They waited as the sun began to sink low in the west, and watched as the ships formed up in convoy and moved past them. They had no rations, no water, and were tired from the day-long maneuvers, They had no desire to spend the night on a mosquito-infested beach.

The ever observant Boudreau, remarked, "*Je penser nous vu embetement.*"

"I think we're screwed."

Finally, as the last boat passed, a Higgins boat came plowing through the surf toward them. They were the only ones left on the beach. If the little boat passed them by it was decided it would be blasted out of the water. The coxswain, perhaps realizing this, revved his engine and ran his little boat up on the beach. The bow ramp dropped with a bang, they climbed aboard, the coxswain raised the ramp, put her in reverse, and took off, full throttle toward the rapidly disappearing ship.

The sea was rough, and rather than settling down at the stern with the bow raised and skimming across the water, like most boats under full power, the fully loaded boat with the squared-off bow ramp, which wasn't elevated enough to skip over the waves, instead plowed right into them. It drove straight against the large waves, and the water began pouring in.

In the gathering darkness, they could see the stern of the last transport far ahead of them. The coxswain made as much speed as possible, and in doing so, more and water came in. Water began filling the bilges below the floor decking, and the coxswain started the pumps to keep them afloat. The troops stood by, prepared to bail with their helmets if necessary. But because of the heavy load, by the time the water rose above the decking, the little boat would probably sink.

It was Rat who remarked, "Now ain't this something? We survive Tarawa and Peleliu, and drown right here in Iron Bottom Bay."

Slowly they gained on the transport, and finally drew up alongside. The ship was packed with marines, and they shouted up to them for help. A Navy officer leaned over the rail and asked them which ship they were from. They told him they had missed their boat, and requested to come aboard. Surely, the Navy guy wouldn't turn them away, would he? He didn't, and gave orders to the coxswain to pull in close. He did so, and two cables with hooks were lowered to them. Just as the hooks were fastened to rings in the floor, the Higgins boat seemed to start sinking. Only the cables held it up. A cargo net was lowered, and the marines scrambled up and aboard the ship.

When they finally rejoined their unit, a man asked, "Where the hell you guys been?"

It was Rat that replied, "We went to Frisco for a beer."

After maneuvers were completed the convoy sailed to where it would join the gathering invasion fleet, which seemed to grow in numbers by the day, finally anchoring off of the island of Ulithi. This time there was no promise of a short operation. Captain Bartholomew told them, "This is expected to be the costliest amphibious landing of the war. We will be hitting an island about 350 miles from the Japanese home islands, so you can expect them to fight with more determination than ever. We can expect

80-85 percent casualties on the beach." Not exactly a morale booster. Thad looked around thinking that eight out of ten men sitting there with him wouldn't make it. Was he one of the eight? One of the two? *Don't think about it.*

The captain continued, "We may have trouble getting over that cliff or seawall in our sector. Also, according to our G-2 there is a large Jap gun placed just on the right flank of our battalion sector. We hope naval gunfire can knock it out. It's pretty certain that the Japs will pull off a massive counterattack, probably supported by tanks, sometime during our first night ashore or just before dawn. They'll *banzai* and try to push us off the beachhead."

"And the good news is?"

On 27 March, the loudspeaker came on with, "Now hear this. Now hear this. Special sea detail stand by." Sailors assigned to the detail moved to their stations, and they weighed anchor.

Tensions mounted on the eve of D-Day. They received final orders to move off the beach as fast as possible. *No problem there. I'll be moving just as fast as, if not faster than the Japs let me.* They were also reminded that even though they were in regimental reserve, they would probably get the hell kicked out of them coming off the beach. They were advised to hit the rack early.

Predawn reveille. It was Easter Sunday, April Fool's Day, 1945. Some April Fool's joke. Their breakfast was steak and eggs, the usual feast before the slaughter. They returned to their compartment and got their gear squared away, Thad checking and double checking his medical pouches. This time he was going in with a carbine *and* his .45. He checked his weapons one last time and deemed himself ready for battle, thinking, *This never gets any easier.* If anything it was harder, knowing he'd been lucky so far. He closed his eyes and offered a short prayer. "Please, Lord, just one more time."

He went into the head to relieve his distressed stomach,

cramped by fear and apprehension, then joined the other men on deck to await orders. They milled around, watching the bombardment of the beach by their warships while the planes joined in strafing, firing rockets, and bombing. Higgins boats would take them to rendezvous areas and transfer them to amtracs, which had previously delivered the assault waves to the beach.

The weather was clear and incredibly cool. They climbed down the cargo net and settled into the Higgins boat. Someone yelled, "Shove off, Coxswain; you're all loaded."

Okinawa
The Last Battle

Beginning in April of 1945, on an island in the Pacific, American and Japanese men fought and killed each other as never before. Caught in the crossfire between these warring powers were the native inhabitants of Okinawa.

During these eighty-two days, over 250,000 people lost their lives, including approximately 150,000 Okinawans, about a third of the population. At the battles end, somewhere between a third and a half of all surviving civilians were wounded. No battle during the Second World War, except Stalingrad, had as massive loss of civilian life. The stakes were high. The Japanese, determined to fight to the last man, almost achieved their objective, but in defeat, 100,000 Japanese combatants died rather than surrender.

United States' loss of life was staggering as well. The United States Navy sustained the largest loss of ships in its history with thirty-six lost and 368 damaged. The Navy also sustained the largest loss of life in a single battle, with almost 5,000 killed and an equal number wounded. At Okinawa, the Tenth Army, a joint task force, initially was made up of 183,000 Army, Navy, and Marine personnel. During those eighty-two days, the Tenth Army would lose 7,613 men.

The operation on Okinawa was named Operation Iceberg. It began on 1, April, 1945, Easter Sunday. The landing would be referred to as "L Day," or "Love Day," and perhaps in keeping with April Fool's Day, the landing encountered virtually no opposition. This lack of opposition was completely unexpected and unprecedented. The Tenth Army was, itself, unique. With the combination of Admiral Chester Nimitz and General Douglas MacArthur's forces, a joint task force had been assembled.

Military units fought bravely on Okinawa. The Tenth Army consisted of ten Army Divisions, including the 77th, the 95th, the 27th, the 81st and the 7th. Three Marine Divisions fought on Okinawa, the 1st, 2nd, and 6th. These divisions were all supported by naval, amphibious, and tactical air forces. If one were telling the story of the Navy on Okinawa, the story would be about kamikazes and the largest loss of life in the U.S. Navy's history.

The Japanese knew they could not win; therefore their mission became a battle of attrition. For every man lost, he must take ten Americans, for every plane, a boat. The objective would be to destroy, or at least delay the U.S. Fleet. This would give the Japanese time to prepare the homeland. The southern end of Okinawa seemed ideal for the Japanese battle of attrition. Honeycombed with caves that had for over a year had been reinforced to create interlocking defenses, the southern end was easily defended. Ridges and rocky embankments, trees and foliage, made it an easy place in which to fight a battle of attrition. Delaying tactics would be employed, hoping for a southern standoff. Meanwhile, the U.S. Fleet would be supplying the troops on land, leaving them exposed to Japanese naval and air attacks. This, argued Tokyo's leaders, would further slow the Allies' attack on the homeland.

The Navy began "softening up" the island on 21 March with naval bombardment. The softening up would make the landing easier for the assault troops when they came ashore. Naval bombardments would remove walls, foliage, and other barriers as well as kill troops. The Okinawans came to refer to the bombardment as the "Typhoon of Steel."

The first waves went in at 0830 on the first day of April. The landings were to take place on the west coast of Okinawa. The plan called for the U.S. forces to spread out and sever the island in two. The expected bloody landing never materialized. The Tenth Army strolled onto the island with little or no opposition.

Equipment and 60,000 troops were onshore by the end of the first day. By the seventh day, L-7, the marines had secured Nago, Okinawa's second largest city, and were headed further north. Organized resistance on the northern two thirds of the island ended on 20 April. The Marine Divisions thought their job finished. Not so fast there, Jarhead.

Word began to filter that things were not going smoothly in the south. The Army had mired down. One of the Army units, the 27th, already had a reputation for having performed poorly in previous island fighting, and now the Marines were being ordered to head south and bail them out.

One problem for the Tenth Army would be the rain, which by 9 May had begun in earnest. Everything became muddy. Moving supplies and equipment proved almost impossible and often had to be accomplished hand-over-hand. Asa Kawa River seemed to be the biggest obstacle between the marines and Naha, the capital of Okinawa. The river would be breached a yard at a time, then all that stood between the marines and Naha were three "insignificant" hills, Half Moon, Horseshoe, and Sugarloaf.

May 12-18 would be filled with some of the most savage fighting in Marine Corps history. The Japanese "Shuri-line" cut the island in half east to west. It consisted of defensive positions, which included mortar, artillery, machine guns, and interconnected tunnel complexes. These tunnels, an estimated sixty miles of interconnected passages, made movement and flanking maneuvers easy for the Japanese. In addition the marines ran into what they referred to as "spider holes," flush with the ground and covered with brush or dirt. These hideaways kept the men constantly vigilant about what might be behind them. The Japanese would lie in wait for a patrol to pass, pop up out of their spider hole, and open fire. The marines found that the Japanese were not going to give up the Shuri-line of defense without a tremendous payment.

Another aspect of the Okinawa campaign was the plight of the civilian campaign. The Okinawans were a docile people of small stature who were faced with an unenviable situation. Caught between the hammer and the anvil, their situation during the war was miserable. The Japanese had told the Okinawan civilians to go south.

Innocent people lost their homes and property due to the American assault. Men had been conscripted to take part in the defense of their island, while women, children, and elders were forced into hiding in the small, underground shelters. They were thrown out of their hiding places as the Japanese retreated and took these caves for themselves. Moreover, girls had devoted themselves to running and cooking for the soldiers and had gone as far to volunteer in carrying ammunition, or joining in attacking the enemy. Very little consideration was given to these noncombatants by their Japanese overlords. At battles' end, one third of the native population had perished.

Not all Okinawans were conscripted. Some were willing

participants. Like all civilians who have been fed wartime propaganda, The Okinawans had unwarranted fears that accounted for their initial resistance and the large number of suicides. Many Okinawans made it clear that they felt they were fighting for their lives against the barbarous Americans, who would rape the women and eat the children. Once the civilians discovered that the Allied troops did not intend to harm them, they surrendered and once again became extremely docile.

Naval personnel responsible for civilian relocation during the battle explained that the Okinawans had been living in caves and were terrified to come out. They were covered in lice and unclean, starved and injured from bombing, shelling, and bullets. Even at the battle's beginning, seventy-five percent of their homes had been destroyed.

The First Okinawan Prefectural Girls School made up the Himeyuri Students Corps. These were the most well-thought-of girls on Okinawa. When the battle began, the Himeyuri girls, numbering roughly 225 and ranging in age from fifteen to nineteen, were used as nurses' aides in the Japanese military hospital. These privileged young ladies usually did the most menial and often the most dangerous work. Thoroughly indoctrinated, most would have it no other way. By 30 May, the Japanese had already lost seventy percent of the forces stationed on Okinawa. At this point, the Army headed south and abandoned these young women. Medical units were deactivated, and the girls were left to their own devices. Pushed out of the caves they moved south, unprepared and unprotected as they tried to find family and protection. By the end of June, just twenty-one remained alive. They have become a symbol on Okinawa of what the Okinawans endured.

The Americans who landed on Okinawa had been briefed regarding the Okinawans, but they quickly surmised for themselves the pitiful situation that they were in. U.S. troops tried to look out for them as best they could. The Okinawans were obviously scared to death, shocked by the bombardment, and after a few days when they realized they wouldn't be hurt, they came out in droves to give themselves up.

The last battle for the marines on Okinawa occurred on 17 June. On 21 June, 1945, the American flag was raised on the southern end of the island. The Battle for Okinawa was over.

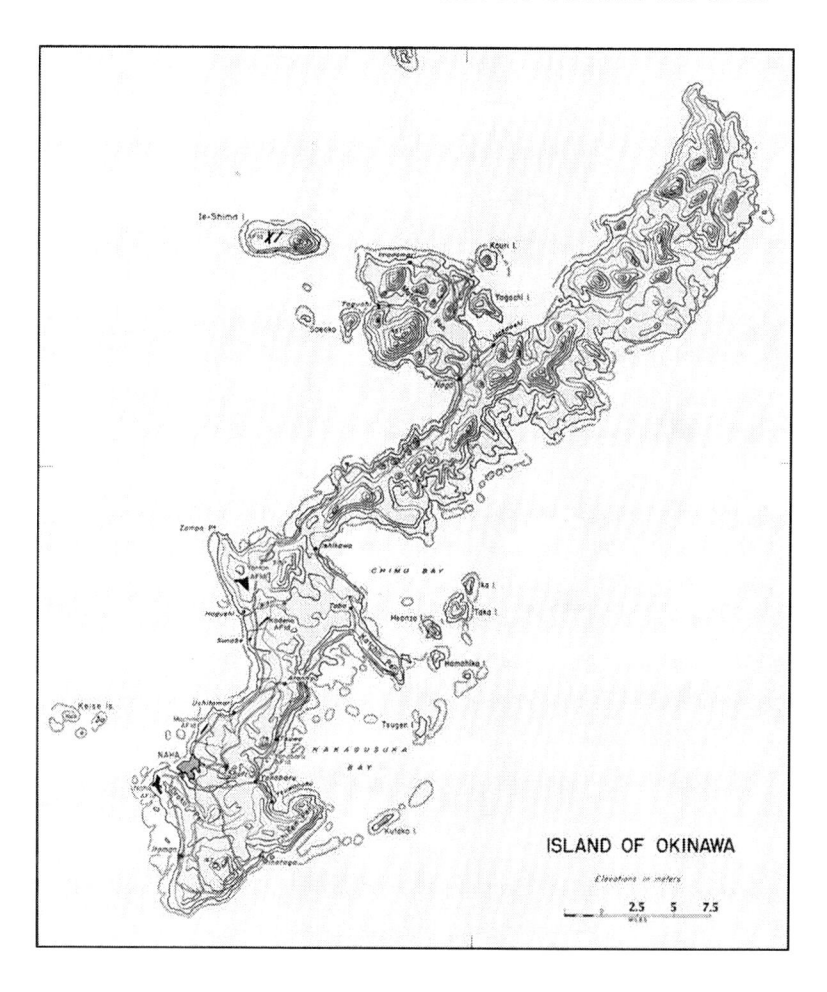

18
1 April 1945

The coxswain gunned the engine and pulled away from the ship. Other boats loaded with marines were pulling out all along the side of the ship. Amphibious craft of every description floated in the water around them. The overwhelming size and magnitude of the invasion was evident.

Thad's boat ran some distance from the ship and began to circle while other boats loaded with men from the battalion began to form up. The bombardment roared on, and sitting low in the water, he couldn't see the beach.

An amtrac returning from delivering marines to the beach pulled alongside. Someone shouted, "The landing is unopposed!"

"The hell, you say."

"I'm telling you late but straight; I ain't seen no casualties. The Japs must have hauled ass. The guys went in standing up."

Everybody started laughing and joking as they made the transfer from the Higgins boat to the little tractor. Thad didn't laugh or joke. He knew better. Common sense told him that only

350 miles from their homeland, they'd defend this island to their death. So they let them walk ashore. Then what?

As they moved closer to the shore they got a good view of the hundreds of landing boats and amtracs approaching the beach. They could see men of their regiment moving ashore with no enemy shells bursting among them. They appeared nonchalant and unhurried, just like maneuvers. *This ain't right.*

The amtrac plowed up onto the beach, the tailgate dropped, and the marines casually picked up their gear and walked out.

They saw the remains of the big gun emplacement that had concerned them in their briefings, and the seawall had been blasted down to a terrace-like rise over which they moved with ease.

They advanced inland, and they neither heard nor saw any Japanese fire directed against them. Jubilation over the lack of opposition to the landing prevailed, especially among the veterans. The replacements began making remarks about amphibious landings being easy. Thad began to relax.

By late afternoon on D-Day they were ordered to dig in for the night. The company set up in a small field that looked like it had been recently plowed. The dirt, rather than coral, made for easy digging in. They were told to expect a counterattack with tanks because of the open nature of the countryside.

Once they were set up and dug in, Garza, Plowboy, Joe Louis Boyd, and Roy Boy went over to the edge of the field and cautiously explored a neat, clean Okinawan farmhouse. It was a likely place for snipers, but they found it empty.

As they were leaving the house to return to their positions, Plowboy stepped on what appeared to be a wooden cover over an underground rainwater cistern at the corner of the house. The wooden planks were rotten, and Plowboy fell through, sinking in above his waist. Poor Plowboy. It wasn't rainwater that he fell into, but sewage from the house, an Okinawan septic tank. He hollered, cussed, and as quickly as possible pulled himself out of the hole. Plowboy smelled worse than a skunk, and for weeks had a hard time finding anyone that would share a foxhole with him.

No sooner had they arrived back at their positions than they heard the unmistakable drone of an airplane engine. They looked up and saw a Japanese Zero directly over them headed toward the fleet offshore. Ships began firing at the plane as he circled and then dove. The engine whined as it headed straight down toward a transport. They saw smoke where the plane had hit the ship, but it was so far away they couldn't determine what damage had been done. It was the first kamikaze they had seen, but it wouldn't be the last.

As darkness began to fall they got squared away for the night. They had each been issued a small bottle containing a few ounces of brandy to ward off the chill of D-Day night. They knew Willis wasn't a drinker and began trying to talk him out of his brandy ration. But the Governor was cold after sundown, and took a small sip of the brandy just to warm him up. It did more than warm him up. It burned all the way down, and he ended up trading his brandy for a can of peaches.

They waited in the clear, chilly night for the expected Japanese attack. When Rat woke Thad up for his turn on watch, he handed him a Tommy gun (a Thompson submachine gun).

"Where the hell did you get this?"

"Doesn't matter where I got it. Just take it, and hope you don't have to use it."

Thad left his carbine, took the Tommy gun, and after a few minutes on watch he noticed what appeared to be a man crouching near him at the edge of some shadows. He stared. He closed his eyes. He opened them and still couldn't be sure, but the harder he looked, the more sure he was that the dark object was a man. He knew it wasn't a marine, because none of his people were placed where the figure was. It was probably an enemy infiltrator waiting for his banzai buddies to get in place before attacking.

He raised the Tommy gun slowly, set it on full automatic, flipped off the safety, took careful aim, and squeezed off a short burst of several rounds. Thad peered confidently over his sights expecting to see a Japanese knocked over by the big .45 slugs. Nothing happened; the enemy didn't move.

Of course, the sound of gun fire in the middle of an otherwise peaceful night, alerted the whole company, some from a sound sleep. There was lot of shouting, "What? Where? How many?"

Thad answered that he thought he had seen a Japanese crouching near the shadows. When dawn broke, it was learned that Thad's infiltrator was a low stack of straw. Rat took back his Tommy gun, telling Thad, "You better let me hang onto this. You might hurt yourself."

On 2 April (D+1), the First Marine Division continued its advance across the island. They moved under the protection of overhead planes, but no artillery support, because no organized body of Japanese had been located ahead of them. "Where the hell are they?" Some scattered small groups were encountered and put up a fight, but the main Japanese army was nowhere to be found.

By the afternoon of 4 April the First Marine Division, moving across the center of the island, had completed their initial task, cutting the island in two. Their rapid movement had been made possible because of the widely scattered opposition. They were confused as to what the Japanese were doing. They knew the Japs weren't going to give up the island without a long, drawn-out fight, and they didn't have to wait long to find out where the enemy was. Army divisions were meeting fierce opposition as they tried to move south, and they heard of another regiment of marines being ambushed just north of them, while the Sixth Marine Division had captured the entire upper part of the island. They were methodically securing chunks and pieces of the island, but where in the hell were the Japs? There were brief skirmishes and firefights, but where was the main body? *I guess we'll find them soon enough. Or they'll find us.*

One morning in mid-April, after a leisurely K-ration breakfast, Thad, Boudreau, and Roy Boy were standing on a ridge watching an air raid on the airfield. As they watched the air raid they heard an airplane engine to their right. They looked down the big valley below the ridge, and here comes a Zero flying up the valley toward them. He slowly cruised by at eye level, no more than thirty of forty yards away. His canopy was open. They saw his leather flying helmet, his goggles pushed up on his forehead, and a white scarf around his neck. As he flew by, he actually grinned at the three marines.

They watched the plane bank and climb to gain altitude and disappear around another ridge. They knew that he would be back, this time to strafe them with no cover in sight. Again they heard the plane. This time it wasn't the throb of a cruising engine, but the roar of a plane at full throttle. The Zero streaked by them going down the valley in the opposite direction from where it had first appeared. He was still flying at eye level, and he was in a big hurry. The reason he was in a big hurry was that a blue Marine Corsair was hot on his tail, and they roared out of sight over the ridge tops.

Ugly rumors began to increase about the difficulties the Army troops were having on southern Okinawa. From high ground on clear nights they could see lights flickering and glowing on the southern skyline. Sometimes they heard a distant rumble. Thad tried to convince himself that it was thunderstorms, but he knew better.

As April wore on rumors and bad news increased about the situation the Army was facing down south. The marines instinctively knew that sooner or later they would be employed there. They finally got word that they would be moving out on 1 May to replace the 27th Infantry Division. They were given instructions and issued ammunition and rations. They boarded trucks and headed south.

19

When they stopped and got off of the trucks they took up a single file on the right side of a narrow road, and began walking south. Ahead they could hear the explosions of mortar and artillery rounds, the rattle of machine guns, and the popping of rifle fire.

Soon a column of men approached from the opposite direction. They were Army infantry from the 106th Regiment, 27th Infantry Division, that they were relieving. They were beat. They were dirty and hollow eyed. Thad had seen the same look on Tarawa and Peleliu. *One more time.*

They left the road and raced across an open field as Japanese shells of all types exploded all around them. Another nightmare. They reached a gentle swale and fell into it, out of breath, panting, frightened. Soldiers that they were relieving were rushing past, trying to get out alive.

Japanese rifle and machine-gun fire increased into a constant rattle. The shelling grew heavier. They began to dig in. The shock of leaving the quiet countryside that morning and rushing into that deadly storm of bullets and explosions was overwhelming. On that first day of May, after a peaceful April, this caught the marines completely off balance, like awakening from a pleasant dream only to find that you're living a nightmare. Thad had been through this before. He knew what to expect. He felt fear but not panic. Experience had taught him what to expect from the enemy guns, and he knew he could control his fear. He knew that all anyone could do under such intense enemy fire was to hug the deck and pray.

At Tarawa and Peleliu Thad had not experienced the munitions that the Japs were throwing at them on Okinawa. Rifle fire, machine-gun fire, little knee mortars, big mortars, light artillery and heavy artillery. *What we need to do is find where they store all that ammunition and bomb it. Good idea, Hayes. Why don't you suggest that to Admiral Nimitz?*

Many men were superstitious about one's chances of surviving a third campaign. By that time one's luck was wearing thin. Thad was contemplating this while treating the gunny's wound. A bullet had ripped off the top portion of his right ear. This was Thad's third battle in what? A year and a half, and he had remained unscathed, except for getting stabbed by Pytel. This was the gunny's third, and he just came within a fraction of an inch of going to that big PX in the sky. Shouting to be heard above the racket, Thad said, "Gonna have to make a few wraps of this around your head, kinda like a turban that them Muslims wear. You ain't a Muslim, are you, Gunny?"

"Nope. But if I have to be a Muslim to make it out of here, you can call me Gunny Muhammad."

While continuing to wrap his head, Thad shouted, "Okay, Muhammad. And I'll tell you what else. There was a famous painter, don't remember his name, cut off his ear. Something about a whore. When you get home, you should try your hand at painting."

"I painted my house once. Does that count?"

"It's a start, Gunny Muhammad. It's a start."

"It's been nice visiting with you, Doc, but don't you think we should be getting our young asses back to work?"

"Good idea."

The calls came: "Corpsman!"

He rushed in a low crouch in the direction of the calls. He passed Garza. He passed half of Garza. His bottom half was gone. *Keep running.* Another marine with no head, still clutching his rifle. He found the Governor in a still smoldering shell crater. Shrapnel had peppered him along his whole left side. He bled from his forehead. Several pieces had entered his chest and stomach. There was no gurgling sound. The Governor clutched his stomach and curled into a tight ball, saying, "Aww, aww, aww, man!"

"Hang on, Gov. I'm going to patch you up and get you out of here."

"It hurts, Doc."

"I know it hurts, but we're going to take care of the hurt right now." Thad gave him a shot of morphine, then he worked on cleansing the wounds, none of which seemed to be life threatening.

By the time he got them cleaned and bandaged, the Governor had made it to that happy place where morphine takes you. "You're right, Doc. It don't hurt no more. How about getting me a ride out of here?"

"Right. I'll see what I can do."

Thad ran to find stretcher bearers. An explosion knocked him off his feet. As he lay there, he realized all his moving parts still moved, so he got up and continued on, found stretcher bearers, and led them back to where the Governor lay. A grinning Governor.

"Here's your ride, Gov. They're going to take you out of here, and you're going to be just fine. You'll be on a hospital ship before you know it."

"Pretty nurses, Doc?"

"You bet."

The shelling seemed to taper off, and the marines began to dig in just below the crest of a low, sloping section of a ridge. The digging was easy in Okinawa's clay-like soil. It was a luxury after the coral rock of Tarawa and Peleliu.

Once Roy Boy started digging a foxhole he didn't seem to know when to quit. He just kept on keeping on. "You get that hole much deeper, they're going to get you for desertion."

"Back home, my mama used to tell me if I dug a hole deep enough, I'd end up in China. I'm thinking that if I dig this one deep enough, I'll end up back in the States. What do you think?"

"Keep digging."

When he finally got his foxhole deep enough, he began laying wooden boards from ammo boxes over the top, leaving just enough opening for him to crawl through. Then he threw about six inches of soil all over the top of the boards. "You going to furnish that thing, Roy Boy? How about curtains? Maybe a throw rug?"

"You guys can laugh now, but when the shelling starts, I'll be the one that's laughing."

"What if a mortar round lands right on top?"

Roy Boy just shook his head and climbed into his foxhole.

Before dark they learned that they would be making a big attack the next morning all along the U.S. line. With the heavy Japanese fire that had been pouring into them, they dreaded the thought of making such a push. Their objective was to reach a stream about 1,500 yards to the south.

With the dawn, came the rain. There was some small arms fire all along the line, and a few artillery shells passed back and forth during the gloomy morning. The rain let up temporarily, and Thad ate some K rations. On the pocket-sized tripod issued to him, he heated up a canteen cup of coffee with a sterno tablet.

As 0900 approached, artillery and ships' guns increased their rate of fire. The rain poured down, and the Japanese answered with their artillery. They started throwing more shells at the marines, most of which passed over their lines and exploded far to their rear where their artillery was emplaced.

The battalion finally received orders to open fire with their mortars and machine guns. The artillery and ships' guns increased in tempo at an awesome rate as the time for the attack approached. The noise increased all along the line. Rain fell in torrents, and the soil became muddy and slippery.

At 0900, the noise that had been loud, became a deafening roar. The riflemen tried to rush forward and barely got out of their foxholes when enemy fire from their front drove them back. These marines coming back to the line all wore wild-eyed, shocked expressions that showed only too vividly that they had barely escaped the carnage that awaited them. They clung to their rifles and BARs and slumped to the mud to pant for breath before moving behind the ridge to their former foxholes. The torrential rain made it all seem so much more unbelievable and terrible. The order was given to cease fire while stretcher bearers rushed out to retrieve the wounded. They, too, became fair game for the Japanese riflemen.

Sergeant Bradley was the last man in, and then he proceeded to rush out to the men pinned down in front of the ridge, where he threw smoke grenades to shield them from the Japanese fire. He returned with a hole shot through his dungaree cap (he wasn't wearing a helmet), and another through his pants' leg. He had been hit in the leg with shell fragments but refused treatment. *One tough dude, that Sergeant Bradley.*

For Thad and the other corpsmen it was going to be a rotten morning, with flesh wounds, chest wounds, limbs torn away. Marines were screaming in pain, some calling for their mothers. Others suffered silently. It didn't take long for the corpsmen to use up their supply of morphine. All Thad could do for the suffering was to treat the wounds, all the while hoping that they would pass out to escape the pain.

The bullets began to slacken as all the men made it back to the cover of the ridge. They crouched in their foxholes in the pouring rain, the enemy gunners pouring fire into the company area to discourage another attack. They were back where they started, having never reached the creek.

Rat, wiping his glasses with the sleeve of his dungaree jacket, said, "Well, that didn't work."

Raymond, the Mouse, ran to their position and told them that the word is that they would remain inactive until the next day. It was Plowboy that suggested, "Say, Mouse, when you get back to company, how about suggesting that we wait till the rain stops? Like maybe next spring."

"I'll be sure to tell him." And with that he was gone again.

The rain had settled into a steady downpour, and every foxhole contained several inches of water. Mud in camp on Pavuvu was a nuisance. Mud on maneuvers was an inconvenience. But mud on a battlefield was misery beyond description.

The shelling finally subsided, and things got fairly quiet, and Thad made it back to the aid station and managed to at least partially refill his two medical pouches, taking as much morphine as allowed.

Back on line he saw stretcher bearers bringing a casualty back through the rain. Instead of turning left behind the ridge, or right behind a ridge further down the line, the team headed straight back between the two low ridges. That was a mistake, because the Japanese could still fire in that area. "Don't do it!"

As the stretcher bearers approached the cover of some trees, the Japanese riflemen opened up on them. Thad saw bullets kicking up mud and splashing in the puddles of water around the team. The four stretcher bearers hurried across the slippery field, but couldn't go faster than a rapid walk, or the casualty might fall off the stretcher.

He watched helplessly as the team struggled across the muddy field with bullets falling all around them. To watch men struggling to save a wounded comrade was absolute agony. To lighten their loads, the four carriers had put all of their personal equipment aside, except for a rifle or carbine over their shoulders. Each held a handle of the stretcher in one hand, leaving the other free for balance. Their shoulders were stooped with the weight of the stretcher, the casualty laying on the narrow canvas stretcher, his life in the hands of the struggling four.

The two carriers in the rear got hit by a burst of fire. Their knees buckled, and they fell backwards onto the muddy ground. The stretcher pitched into the mud. The two marines at the other end of the stretcher immediately threw it down, spun around and grabbed the casualty between them. Then each supported a wounded carrier with his other arm. They limped and struggled into the cover of some bushes, bullets still kicking up mud all around them.

Thad rushed to treat the casualty. He was dead. The two wounded stretcher bearers both suffered leg wounds. They were treated and helped to safety by the other two stretcher bearers.

Before nightfall the company received information that they would push again the next day. As the rain slowly diminished and then ceased they made their grim preparations.

While receiving extra ammo, rations, and water, Thad

managed to complete filling his medical pouches and saw the company officers and NCOs gathering nearby. They stood or squatted around Captain Bartholomew, talking quietly, giving orders and answering questions. The officers and NCOs all had had serious, sometimes worried expressions as they listened. Those in the ranks watched their familiar faces carefully for any sign of what was in store for them.

After the CO dismissed his junior officers, they returned to their respective platoons and briefed the men about the next morning's push. They were assured that they would receive maximum support from heavy artillery.

The marines were partially successful in that day's attack. The Japanese heavy machine guns had been knocked out by mortars the previous day, and that helped the company advance to the next low ridge line, but they couldn't hold. They were driven back about a hundred yards by heavy machine-gun fire. They only gained about three hundred yards for the entire day.

They moved into a quiet area back of the front lines well before dark. Word came that because of heavy casualties over the past two days fighting, the company would go into battalion reserve for a while. They dug in around the battalion aid station for its defense.

The company settled into their holes for the night, feeling more at ease off the line and in a quiet area, confident that they would have a fairly quiet night. Not to be. Thad had barely dropped off to sleep, when Joe Louis Boyd woke him with, "Wake up, Doc. The Japs are up to something."

Startled, he awoke and instinctively unholstered his .45 and laid his carbine across his lap.

The voice of an NCO said, "Stand by for a ram, you guys. One-hundred-percent alert!"

Then the next order came: "Stand by for possible Jap paratroop attack. All hands turn to. Keep your eyes open."

"Just what we need, but they can't be any worse than the Jap infantry." The fear was that they would land behind them, forcing the marines to fight from the front as well as their rear, possibly being surrounded. Most nights they had to keep a sharp lookout right, left, front, and rear. That night they had to scan even the dark sky for parachutes.

The marines lived constantly with the fear of death or maiming from wounds, but the possibility of being surrounded by the enemy and wounded beyond the ability to defend themselves was always in the back of their minds. The Japanese were notorious for their brutality.

A couple of Japanese planes flew over during the night, but they passed without dropping parachutes. They were fighters or bombers on their way to attack the ships off shore.

There was a great of deal artillery fire to the company's left, which roared on and on with frightening intensity, drowning out the rattle of machine guns and rifle fire. To their left, small-arms and mortar fire, and scattered rifle fire to their rear. Gunny Mancillas figured this was no more than rear echelon guys firing at shadows. Nonetheless, it was a long night made worse by the uncertainty and confusion all around them.

At first light they heard planes attacking the ships and could see the fleet throwing up antiaircraft fire. They learned that during the night, hundreds of Japanese had been slaughtered in the water trying to infiltrate behind the division. The major threat was over, and they were told that the division would re-locate to the center of the American line.

20

Ammunition, boxes of rations, and five-gallon cans of water were being brought up as close to the front as possible, but because of the mud, all of the supplies were piled across a draw, about fifty yards to the rear. Plowboy, Roy Boy, and Joe Louis Boyd joined the detail to carry the supplies from the dump up to the line where they were dug in.

After making a couple of trips a light machine gun opened up from their left. They were about half way across, in no particular hurry, and at the first burst of fire, took off at a run, slipping and sliding in the mud, to the protected area where the supply dump was placed. Slugs were pinging all around them. The enemy machine gunner was well concealed and had a clear field of fire anytime anyone crossed, yet they had to get the ammunition distributed for the coming attack.

They looked across the draw and saw Sergeant Bradley throw a phosphorus grenade to give them smoke screen protection when they came back across. He threw several more grenades. Thick clouds of white, thick smoke hung in the air. The three marines picked up cases of ammunition, and prepared to cross. The machine gun kept firing down the smoke-covered draw.

Reluctantly, they took off at intervals while the sergeant was throwing more phosphorus grenades to cover them.

The smoke hid them from the gunner, but he kept firing short bursts down the draw to prevent their crossing. With slugs popping all around them, expecting to be hit at any time, they made it across. They dropped the heavy ammo boxes in the mud and took cover behind the knoll joining Sergeant Bradley. They thanked him, but he seemed more occupied with solving the problem at hand than talking.

Just then they heard the engine of a tank some distance across the draw. Without hesitation, Sergeant Bradley took off across the draw toward the sound. *There goes Superman.*

He made it across safely. Through the smoke they could see him make contact with the tank. Then, they saw him backing toward them slowly, directing the big Sherman tank with hand signals across the draw. The machine gunner kept firing blindly as the tank finally reached them.

The tankers had agreed to act as a shield for the marines in their hazardous crossings. They crouched beside the tank, always with it between them and the machine gun, which was no longer firing. They kept this up until all the ammunition was safely across, and the tank rumbled off in the direction of the Japanese machine gun.

On 9 May word was passed, "Prepare for full frontal attack." Ammunition had been issued, and the marines busied themselves squaring away their gear, adjusting cartridge belts, rifle slings, and pack straps, saying silent prayers. These little gestures of no value other than releasing tension in the face of the impending terror.

Thad, whose orders were to stay back and assist at the aid station, studied the faces of his friends. He remembered a poem he learned in high school: *Cannon to the right of them, cannon to the left of them, cannon in front of them volleyed and thundered; Stormed at with shot and shell, boldly they rode and well. Into the jaws of death, into the mouth of hell rode the six hundred.*

The ground had dried, at least sufficiently for the tanks to maneuver, and they stood by, engines idling, hatches open, and the tankers waiting, waiting like everyone else. Men sat silently, lost in their own thoughts.

The pre-assault bombardment commenced. The big shells roared overhead from each battery of their artillery, while the big guns from the ships began to shell the enemy defenses ahead of them. Then came the planes: Corsairs and dive bombers firing rockets, dropping bombs, and strafing.

Enemy artillery and mortar rounds began coming in as the Japanese tried to disrupt the attack, and then the order came to "Stand by." The air strike ended, and the artillery and the ship's guns slacked off. The tanks and riflemen moved out, and things went well for a couple of hundred yards before heavy fire from the Japanese stopped the attack. The riflemen were catching hell. The bloody, dazed and wounded were being carried or were walking to the aid station in the rear. There Thad, other corpsmen, and doctors were doing their best to care for them, patch them up so they could rejoin the fray, or set them aside to wait for transportation to the beach and onto the off-shore hospital ships. The dead were laid outside of the tent and covered with ponchos.

The assault, if you can call it that, stalled. Thad, thought, *At two hundred yards a day, we'll be here forever or until there's no one left to fight. Whichever comes first. Are we demanding too much from these brave young men?* Theirs not to reason why, theirs but to do or die; into the valley of death rode the six hundred.

Charlie Company had fallen back, and their sector remained relatively quiet during the night. Thad had rejoined the company and was sharing a foxhole with Rat. While preparing their K rations, he noticed one of the lenses of Rat's eye glasses was cracked. "I hope that's not your shooting eye. What happened?"

"A little piece of shrapnel, I guess. Hadn't been for my glasses, might have lost my eye. It is my shooting eye, and it's a little late to learn how to shoot left handed. I lost my Thompson somewhere out there, so I'm going to get me a BAR, so all I have to do is set that sucker on full automatic and spray and pray."

"How'd you lose the Thompson?"

"Ran out of ammo. Had to throw it at a Jap before the Cajun shot him. Another Jap picked up the Tommy gun and took off with it. Boudreau said he thinks he hit him, but he ain't sure. A thieving Jap. Can't trust 'em."

"I got, it Rat. Wear your glasses upside down."

"Fuck you."

It was just before dawn when the order came. "Stand by, you guys. Get ready to move out. The Japs are counterattacking, and we're on standby to go up and stop 'em." They picked up their gear and moved wearily back toward the front.

When they reached the marines that had been under attack, they found the situation to be secure. The attack had been repulsed as evidenced by the number of Japanese bodies strewn across the battlefield. "About face. We're moving back." Their help wasn't needed, so it was back through the mud and rain they went.

All movements during the month or May and early June were physically exhausting and exasperating because of the mud. Typically they moved in single file, keeping the five paces apart, slipping and sliding up and down muddy slopes and through boggy fields. When the column slowed or stopped, the tendency was to bunch up, and they had to be reminded, "Keep the five-pace interval. Don't bunch up." The ever present danger of enemy fire made it necessary to stay strung out. However, sometimes when it was too dark, in order not to get separated and lost each man was ordered to hold onto the cartridge belt of the man in front of him. This made for tough sledding over rough and muddy terrain. Many times a man would slip and fall, taking others with him.

It seemed that every time they stopped, the order came, "Move out!"

The column always moved forward but like a rubber band being stretched, or like an accordion being compressed, then strung out, stopping and starting. The natural inclination was for a man to put down his gear every time they stopped, maybe even sit on his helmet, but just as soon as he did, the order came again, "Move out." Fatigue, at least temporarily, became the number-one enemy. It drove the men to a state of frustration and exasperation.

Wana Draw

Wana Draw aimed like an arrow into the heart of the Japanese defenses, a natural avenue of approach. The marines knew this. The Japanese knew this and took advantage. It couldn't have provided a better opportunity for their defense if they had designed it. The longest and bloodiest battle for Okinawa now faced the men of the First Marine Division. The attack against the "Draw" began on 15 May.

The tanks first, firing their .75 mm cannon, thoroughly shelled the draw. They slowly advanced but received such heavy Japanese fire in return that the riflemen assigned to attack with the tanks had to seek any protection they could in ditches and holes while they covered the tanks from a distance. The fire was such that no man standing could have survived the fire that the enemy was throwing at the tanks. And the tanks couldn't move safely beyond the cover the riflemen provided because of Japanese suicide-tank-destroyer teams. After suffering some hits, the tanks finally pulled back. Rat, waiting, watching with the others, commented, "Well, that didn't work. Wonder if we've got a plan B?"

Artillery and naval gunfire threw up a barrage at the Japanese positions around the draw, followed by an air strike. The bombardment of the draw seemed very heavy to the marines, but it wasn't anything compared to what was to become necessary before the draw was taken.

The company was told to spread out, take cover, and await further instructions. Some found holes. Others scooped out what they could while Japanese shells began exploding not far from them. There was a shout for a corpsman. Doc Johnson, Baker Company corpsman, got hit.

When Thad reached him several other marines were with Doc Johnson, who was lying back in the fox hole. He looked up at Thad as he bent over him. While bandaging his neck wound, Thad asked him how he was doing. A really stupid question. He opened his lips to speak, and blood trickled out from between them. Thad was afraid that vital blood vessels in his neck had been severed, and didn't see how he could possibly survive.

He took Johnson's hand. "Don't talk, Doc. I'm going to get you out of here, and you'll be okay."

After doing all he could for Doc Johnson, he stood up. "Okay, you guys, get him out of here."

The massive artillery, mortar, naval gunfire, and aerial bombardment continued against the draw to their front and Wana Ridge on their left. The Japanese continued to shell everything and everyone in the area, meeting each tank, and infantry attack with a storm of fire. A total of thirty tanks, including four flame-thrower tanks, blasted and burned the draw.

The thunderous American barrages went on and on for hours and then days. In return, the Japanese threw plenty of ordnance at the marines. It didn't seem possible for any human being to be under such thunderous chaos for days and nights on end and be unaffected by it. How did the Japanese stand up under it?

They simply remained deep in their caves until it stopped and then came out and returned fire. Somehow, the heavy guns and air strikes had to knock down, knock out or cave in the enemy's well-constructed defensive positions.

After days of fighting, the company finally reached what they supposed was the mouth of the draw itself. Now they waited in an open field, awaiting the order to move across. They eased up to the edge of the draw to cross in groups of three or four. An NCO ordered Thad, Rat, Joe Louis Boyd, and one other to cross directly across the draw. The other side looked mighty far away, especially with Japanese machine guns firing down the draw.

"Haul ass, and don't stop for anything until you get across!" They left the field and slid down a ten-foot embankment to the sloping floor of the draw. Their feet hit the deck running, a three-hundred-yard dash.

The Japanese machine guns rattled away. Bullets zipped and snapped all around them. Tracers were long white streaks. The men splashed across a little stream and dashed up the slope to the shelter of a spur of the ridge projecting out into the draw.

Once behind the spur, Thad was out of the line of machine gun fire. He glanced back to see that everyone made it. Rat almost made it. About fifty yards shy of the promised land, curled in a ball, he was holding one leg. Thad called out to him. With all the racket, there was no way Rat could hear him. Thad knew he had to go back out and get him.

Suddenly, Joe Louis Boyd dashed out, scooped up Rat like a steam shovel grabbing up a hunk of dirt. In one motion, he picked up Rat and headed back to the ridge. He landed, rolling Rat over the top of him to cushion the fall.

Thad reached for Rat's leg, and he protested, "I'm all right. Leave me alone."

"What do you mean you're all right? You been hit."

Thad searched along the leg that Rat had been holding. A burst of machine gun fire interrupted his effort. He lay flat for a moment and grabbed the leg again.

Rat seemed in deep pain, and told Joe Louis Boyd, "Thanks for getting me, man, I mean it." He pushed his glasses back to the top of his nose. "Now." He reached tentatively for his foot. "I think I caught a round in my toe."

Thad smiled. "In your toe?"

"You think it's funny? Shoot yourself in the foot, and see how it feels." He began to unlace his boot. He grimaced as he started to pull his boot off, told Thad to get a battle dressing ready. In one painful yank, he pulled the boot off.

There was no blood. The sock was dry. All toes were present and accounted for.

"Take the sock off, Rat."

"Don't need to."

"Sure you do. Come on. Take it off."

"I don't need to, Doc. All right?" Rat found the bottom of his sock finding a tear in it that was perhaps an inch long. "Gimme my boot."

"You mean after all that, you ain't even wounded?"

"The boot, Doc. All right?"

Thad reached behind him where Rat had thrown the boot, and handed it to him. Rat examined it carefully, feeling the bottom of the boot with one hand. He shook his head in disbelief. "Look at that, will you? Check this out." The heel of the boot was gone, there was a small hole where the bullet had entered. There was no exit hole. "Somewhere inside this boot is a bullet." He stuck his foot in the air showing them the torn sock

Joe Louis Boyd looked at the boot with the missing heel and the tear in the sock. "Nahhh. I don't believe it."

Rat laughed, relieved. "I'm telling you late but straight; it felt like someone put a whack on my foot with a damn sledgehammer. Damn near turned a flip. Landed on my ass."

Joe Louis Boyd nodded. "You should call in a Purple Heart for that man. Yep. Definitely worth a Heart."

Rat, still laughing, said, "No blood. Not a drop. Forget it."

Thad, Joe Louis Boyd, and Rat slowly made their way back to the line, Rat limping slightly, Thad shaking his head.

21

They made it up the slope and made contact with that portion of the company that had made it across. There were some still on the other side of the draw awaiting their turn to cross. Gunny told Thad, "We got a kid over there that just got hit. Can you guys get him out?" He pointed out the location of the casualty.

Thad, Rat, and Joe Louis Boyd sent the fourth man to get a stretcher. They moved along the ridge into some brush, where they found the wounded marine. As they came up he said, "Man, am I glad to see you guys."

"You hit bad?" Thad asked as he knelt down beside him.

"Be careful. Japs right over there in those bushes."

Rat and Joe Louis Boyd unslung their rifles and kept an eye on where he indicated, while Thad talked to him. "Where you hit?"

"Right here," he said, pointing to the lower right portion of his abdomen.

He was talkative and seemed in no pain. He was obviously in shock, and Thad knew he would hurt badly soon enough. There was a smear of blood around a tear in his dungaree trousers, so Thad unhooked his cartridge belt and then his belt and opened his trousers to see how serious the wound was. It wasn't the round neat hole of a bullet, but a ragged, nasty gash, characteristic of a shell fragment. It was about two inches long. It oozed a small amount of blood.

While applying sulfa powder and preparing a pressure bandage, Thad asked, "What hit you?"

"Our company sixty mortars," answered the wounded marine. "It was my own damn fault that I got hit, though. We were ordered to halt back there a ways and wait while the mortars shelled this area. But I saw a damn Jap and figured if I got a little closer I could get a clear shot at the sonofabitch. When I got here, the mortars came in, and I got hit. Guess I'm lucky it ain't worse. On top of that, the damn Jap got away."

"You just take it easy now," Thad said as the stretcher came up.

They put the young marine on the stretcher, put his rifle and helmet alongside him, and moved back down the ridge a little way to a deep ravine cut into the ridge, where several corpsmen and a doctor were working. It had sheer walls and a level floor and was perfectly protected. About a dozen wounded, stretcher cases and walking wounded were already there.

As they laid their casualty on the floor of the ravine Thad told him, "You're in good hands now. You're going to be just fine."

"Thanks a lot, you guys. Good luck." They wished him luck and a quick trip to the States.

The four of them split up, moved apart a little and looked for shelter along the slope to await orders. Thad found the perfect two-man standing foxhole with a perfect view of the draw for a long distance right and left. Obviously, it had been used as a defensive position against any movement in the draw and probably had sheltered a couple of Japanese riflemen or perhaps a machine gun. But the hole and its surroundings were devoid of any enemy equipment or trash of any kind. No empty cartridge cases or ammo cartons.

The Japanese had become so security conscious they not only removed their dead, but sometimes even picked up their expended brass, just like the marines did on the rifle range. Sometimes all they found were blood stains on the ground where one had been killed or wounded. They removed everything they could when possible to conceal their casualties. When they even removed their empty cartridge cases, the marines got an eerie feeling, like they were fighting a phantom army.

The marines improvised a creative method for dislodging Japanese defenders from their reverse-slope positions in Wana Draw. Lieutenant Pond led a detail in five hours of muddy backbreaking work. The troops manhandled several drums of napalm (jellied gasoline) up the north side of the ridge. There the marines split the barrels open, tumbled them down into the gorge, and set them ablaze by dropping white phosphorus grenades in their wake. But each small success seemed to be undermined by the Japanese ability to reinforce and resupply their positions during darkness, usually screened by mortar barrages or small-unit counterattacks. The fighting in such close quarters was vicious and deadly. Throughout the period 11-30 May, the division would lose two hundred marines for every one hundred yards advanced.

The weather turned cloudy on 21 May, and the rains began. By midnight the drizzle became a deluge. It was the beginning of a ten-day period of torrential rains. The weather was chilly, and mud was the order of the day. The marines slipped and slid along the trails with every step they took. The division's sector contained no roads. LVTs were committed to delivering ammunition and extracting casualties, and replacement drafts were used to hand-carry food and water to the front lines. This proved less than satisfactory. "You can't move it all on foot." Marine torpedo bombers began dropping supplies by parachute, even though low ceilings, heavy rains, and enemy fire made for hazardous duty. The division commander did everything in his power to keep his troops supplied, reinforced, and motivated, but conditions were extremely grim.

While the First Marine Division was fighting the costly, heartbreaking battle against the Wana positions, The Sixth Marine Division had been fighting a terrible battle for Sugar Loaf Hill, a lump of ground shaped like a loaf of bread. Wana and Sugar Loaf both turned out to be mankillers. Gains were measured by yards won, lost, then won again.

After moving out on the 21st, Charlie Company moved into an area that was the worst that Thad had ever seen on a battlefield, and they stayed there more than a week. The Japanese dead scattered about were numerous.

When they had dug in near enemy dead and conditions permitted, they shoveled muddy soil over them in a vain effort to cut down on the stench and to control the swarming flies. The prolonged artillery and mortar fire made it impossible for the marine units to bury the enemy dead.

They saw that it also had been impossible to remove many marine dead. They laid where they had fallen, an uncommon sight. It was a strong marine tradition to move their dead, even at considerable risk, to an area where they could be covered with a poncho and later collected by the graves registration people. But efforts to remove many marines killed in the area had been in vain. A sad, unavoidable situation.

Thad had heard and read that combat troops in many wars became hardened and insensitive to the sight of their own dead. He found that not to be the case. The sight of a dead Japanese didn't bother him in the least, but the sight of marine dead brought forth regret, never, ever indifference.

Half Moon Hill

While the artillery whined overhead in both directions, the marines of Charlie Company moved to their new positions in the westernmost extension of Wana Draw. They eased into a barren, muddy, shell-torn ridge named Half Moon Hill, and into the foxholes of the company they were relieving. Half Moon was crescent shaped, and the battalion line stretched along the crest of the ridge, with the Japanese occupying caves on the reverse slope.

To their front were the higher, smoke-shrouded Shuri Heights, the heart of the Japanese defensive system. This terrain feature was constantly under bombardment of varying intensity from marine artillery, heavy mortars, and gunfire support ships, as well as being under attack by the infantrymen of the Sixth Marine Division. No matter. It didn't seem to deter the enemy observers from directing their artillery and heavy mortars in shelling Thad's area frequently, every day and every night.

The company CP was situated in a sunken railroad bed. A tarpaulin was stretched over the CP from one side of the railroad embankment to the other. This kept the post snug and dry while torrents of chilly rain kept shivering riflemen, machine gunners, mortarmen, and corpsmen soaked, cold, and miserable day and night in open foxholes.

The almost-continuous downpour that started on 21 May turned Wana Draw into a sea of mud and water that resembled a lake. Tanks bogged down, and even amtracs could not negotiate the slop. Living conditions on the front lines were pitiful. Supply and evacuation problems were severe. Food, water, and ammunition were scarce. Foxholes had to be bailed out constantly. Clothing, shoes, feet and bodies remained constantly wet. Sleep was nearly impossible. The mental and physical strain took a mounting toll on the marines.

Making an almost impossible situation worse were the deteriorating bodies of marines and Japanese that lay just outside the foxholes. Flies multiplied and amoebic dysentery broke out. The First Marine Division would live and fight in this hell for ten days.

After digging in, Thad had his first opportunity to look around. It was the most ghastly corner of hell he had ever witnessed. The area at one time must have been picturesque. Now it was choked with the putrefaction of death, decay, and destruction. In a shallow ditch to his right, lay about twenty dead marines, each on a stretcher and covered to his ankles with a poncho. Those bodies had been placed there to await transport to the rear for burial. Thad thought that at least they were protected from the torrential rains that had made them miserable in life. Looking further, he saw that other marine dead couldn't be tended to properly. The whole area was pocked with shell craters, and every crater was half full of water and many of them held a marine corpse. The bodies lay half submerged in muck, rusting weapons still in hand. Swarms of flies hovered around them.

"Why aren't those guys covered with ponchos?" said Boudreau. The answer came soon enough. Japanese artillery came whistling and whining into the area. He and Thad cowered in their hole as the explosions thundered around them. The enemy gunners in the hills above them were registering their artillery and mortars on their position. They quickly learned that anytime any one of them moved out of their holes the shelling began immediately. They had a terrible time getting the wounded evacuated through the shell fire and mud without the stretcher bearers getting hit. It became perfectly clear why the marine dead were left where they had fallen.

In addition to the marine dead, were the Japanese corpses killed in the heavy fighting that were strewn all around them up to and all over Half Moon. The scene was nothing but mud, explosions, flooded craters with their silent, rotting occupants, knocked-out tanks and amtracs, and discarded equipment: utter, complete, total desolation. There were times on Tarawa and Peleliu that Thad knew it couldn't get any worse. He was wrong.

The stench of death was overpowering. The only way Thad could bear the horror of it all was to look up into the grey sky and repeat over and over to himself that the situation was no more than a nightmare, and he would awake and be somewhere else. He existed from moment to moment, sometimes thinking that death would have been preferable.

Bringing up ammunition from the rear, struggling through the mud, were Plowboy and Shotgun, one of the replacements; his name was Cannon but he wasn't big enough to be a cannon, so they called him Shotgun. They passed near the company CP. "Look at that," said Plowboy. "Captain Bartholomew is in bad shape."

There was the CO just outside the edge of the tarpaulin, trying to stand by himself, but he had to be supported by a man on each side. He looked haggard and weary and was shaking violently. He could barely hold up his head, and the men supporting him seemed to be arguing with him. He was objecting the best he could, but it was a feeble effort because he was so sick.

He had malaria. There was nothing Thad or the doctor could do other than send him back to the aid station. Captain Bartholomew didn't want to be evacuated, but he was so weak he had no choice. Lieutenant Pond would take over. The captain's evacuation ended an era for Thad and several of the others.

Shortly after Lieutenant Pond took over the company, he

promoted Rat and Roy Boy to corporal, and made them squad leaders. *A good choice*, thought Thad. The were both respected veterans and were well thought of throughout the company.

At daybreak the morning after they had taken over the line on Half Moon, Thad went behind a scrawny bush to relieve himself. No sooner had he dropped his pants and squatted than in front of him he saw a sprawled Japanese. The sprawling body's rifle was pointed straight at him, perhaps five yards away. *This ain't no corpse, and I'm in serious trouble.* The eyes behind the rifle were open, glaring into his. Unarmed, Thad thought, *At least let me pull my pants up.*

The two men stared quietly at each other, separated by what seemed only inches, two strides, at most. The man watched Thad, and he stared back waiting for the blast from the rifle that was aimed at his stomach.

The blast rang out from Thad's right. The Jap slumped to his side, dead. The gunny walked up to the body and pumped six more rounds into it, then knelt next to it. He looked up at Thad, who was breathing rapidly.

"Damn, Gunny. The man had me cold. Why didn't he pull the trigger?"

"Because he liked you. Besides, he was out of ammo. Pull up your pants. You look ridiculous."

As the dawn light grew brighter, the lay of the land could be seen through the drizzle and fog, so the mortar section registered their guns with an aiming stakes on three important terrain features. The guns were registered on the reverse slope of Half Moon.

No sooner than the mortars had been registered, they got a reaction. All hell broke loose. Japanese mortar shells began crashing along the crest of the ridge. They came so thick and fast they knew an entire enemy mortar section on Shuri Heights was firing on them. It was not just a solitary gun. They were zeroed in, and it was an awful pounding. Several men were wounded badly. They were moved behind the ridge with great difficulty because of the slippery, muddy slopes. Thad bandaged them, gave them aid, and they were carried to the rear, shocked, torn, and bleeding.

An uneasy quiet then settled along the line. Suddenly someone yelled, "There goes one!" A single Japanese soldier dashed out of the blackness of a culvert at the railroad bed. He carried a bayoneted rifle and a full pack. He ran into the open, turned, and headed for shelter behind the slope of the ridge. It looked as though he had about a thirty-yard dash to make. He didn't. Rat opened up with his BAR, his new weapon of choice, and the soldier fell before he reached the shelter of the ridge.

As the day wore on more Japanese ran out of the culvert in ones and twos and dashed for the shelter behind the slope of the ridge. When they ran out of the culvert, marines fired on them and always knocked them down. The riflemen, BARmen, and machine gunners looked on it as target practice. They were receiving no return fire. Finally they stopped coming, and the Japanese mortars were quiet.

During the lull in firing, Thad walked over to the foxhole that Shotgun was sharing with Boudreau. He learned that Shotgun was from a small town in Louisiana, but to Boudreau's dismay, was not a Cajun. While Thad sat on the edge of the foxhole, Boudreau was lecturing Shotgun in French.

Shotgun looked at Thad, and finally told the coon ass to "Shut the fuck up!"

"I'm trying to make you an honorary Cajun, but you won't listen."

"How can I listen when you're not even talking English?"

"*Pardonnez—moi l'expression.* That's how you learn, *mon cher.* Obviously, you are not willing to learn, or you are not too bright."

Thad said, "How about if he learns all the words to 'Jole Blon'? I bet there are some Cajuns who don't know all the words."

"What the hell is 'Jole Blon'?"

"What the hell is Jole Blon? *Mon dieu!* There is no hope for this man."

Thad said, "Jole Blon' is a Cajun song. Roy Acuff made a record of it."

"Who's Roy Acuff?"

Thad looked at Boudreau. "You're right. There's no hope."

"Obviously, my *estupida ami*, you have led a very sheltered life. Roy Acuff is a popular country singer. But he sings 'Jole Blon' in English. You're going to learn it in French."

"Right."

"Okay. We begin. After me. *'Jole Blon, ma cher 'tit fille...'*"

Thad left them, the Cajun and his "stupid" friend, knowing that in spite of the death and destruction that surrounded them, some were going to emerge without the scars that most would carry for the rest of their lives. *God bless 'em.*

22

After so many months in a world of explosions and people bleeding, suffering, dying, or rotting in the mud, Thad began to wonder if there really was a place in the world where this wasn't happening. He felt a sense of desperation that his mind was being affected by what he was experiencing. Men were cracking. He had seen it many times. They called it combat fatigue.

He made a pledge to himself. The Japanese might wound him or kill him, but they wouldn't make him crack up. His secret resolve helped him make it through the long days and nights he remained in hell. But there were times at night during that period when he felt he was slipping. More than once his imagination ran wild during the brief periods of darkness when the flares and the star shells burned out.

"There comes another one!" More enemy soldiers were rushing out of the culvert. The line started firing as Thad counted the tenth Japanese to emerge. Were they incredibly brave, or so dedicated to their emperor that they were sacrificing themselves right there? Right now? They formed a skirmish line with a few yards between each other, and started trotting silently toward the marines across open ground about three hundred yards away. Their effort was admirable but hopeless. They had no supporting fire of any kind to pin the marines down or even make them cautious. They looked like they were on maneuvers. They had no chance. Zip. Zero. Nada.

Thad stood up with his carbine and started squeezing off rounds. The Japanese held their rifles at port arms and didn't even fire at them. Everyone along the line was yelling and firing. The enemy soldiers had full battle gear with packs, which meant that they had rations and extra ammunition. These were obviously fresh troops, and this might be the beginning of a counter attack of some size.

Within seconds, eight of the ten enemy soldiers pitched forward, spun around or slumped to the deck, dead where they fell. The remaining two must have thought, *This ain't working out too good.* They turned around and started back toward the culvert. Some slacked their fire and just watched. Several men kept firing at the two remaining Japs but missed, and it looked as though they might get away. Finally one Japanese fell forward near a shallow ditch, and the surviving soldier kept going.

Just as one of the machine gunners was zeroing in on him, the order came to cease fire, but the machine gun was making so much noise the order went unheard, and bullets struck the fleeing Japanese in the middle of his pack. The Japanese dropped his rifle as the slugs tore into him, and knocked him face down in the mud. He didn't move.

The enemy soldier who fell near the ditch began crawling and flopped into it. Some of the men started firing at him again. The bullets kicked up mud all around the soldier as he slithered desperately along in the shallow ditch which didn't quite hide him. Machine gun tracers ricocheted off the ground as the Japanese struggled along the shallow ditch.

Then on one of the rare occasions where Thad ever saw compassion expressed of the Japanese by a marine who had to fight them, one of the men yelled, "Knock it off, you guys. The poor bastard's hit, and he's going to die anyway."

"You stupid jerk. He's a Jap, ain't he?"

The firing continued, and bullets hit their mark. The wounded Japanese died in the muddy little ditch. He and his comrades had done their best. "They died gloriously on the field of honor for the emperor," is what their families would be told. In reality their lives were wasted on a muddy, stinking slope for no good reason. And so it goes.

The rains became so heavy that at times the marines could barely see their buddies in the neighboring foxhole. They had to bail out their foxholes with their helmets after each and every downpour, or they filled with water.

Thad and Plowboy had dug a deep foxhole and placed pieces of wooden ammo crates across braces set on the muddy clay at the bottom. At one end they dug a deeper hole to catch the runoff. As surface water poured into the foxhole and under the boards, they bailed out the sump for a day or two. But the soil became so saturated that the four sides of the foxhole leaked like a sieve. It was hard to keep up, but the sump and the board floor kept them out of the water and mud.

The Japanese infantry kept up their activity to their front and tried to infiltrate the lines every night, sometimes with success. One day, as dawn was breaking, Plowboy woke up Thad with, "Halt, who goes there? What's the password?"

Fully awake now, Thad grabbed his carbine and aimed it at two dim figures striding along about twenty yards away. Visibility was so poor in the dim light, mist, and rain that he could tell little about the shadowy figures other than they wore U.S. helmets. At the sound of Plowboy's challenge, the two men speeded up instead of halting and identifying themselves.

"Halt, or I'll fire!" he yelled.

The two took off for the railroad bed as fast as they could on the slippery ground. Plowboy fired several shots with his M-1, but missed. Then they heard a couple of grenades explode in the railroad bed. Then a marine yelled that the Japanese had been killed by his grenades. With the coming of daylight, Thad and Plowboy went over to the railroad embankment to see what had happened. They took a look at the dead enemy before returning to their foxhole. They had been wearing Marine helmets but otherwise were dressed in Japanese uniforms. A grenade had exploded in the face of one. There was no face and little head remaining. The other wasn't so badly mangled, but just as dead.

They returned to their foxhole just in time to see Sergeant Bradley come walking from the company CP. He was stopping at every foxhole along the way to find out who had been so negligent as to let the Japanese soldiers get past them and almost to the CP. He arrived at Thad's and Plowboy's foxhole and asked why they hadn't seen the two soldiers pass if one of them was on watch as they were supposed to be.

Plowboy explained to the sergeant what had happened, and finally Sergeant Bradley said, "Next time, you better not miss." He turned and stalked back to the CP.

The number of casualties during the stalemate at Half Moon were mounting. Most of the wounds resulted from enemy shell fragments, while there were many injuries from blast concussion. This was understandable because of the frequent heavy shellings. Some of the concussion cases could walk and were helped to the rear like men walking in their sleep. Some wore wild-eyed expressions. Others wore expressions of idiots knocked too senseless to be afraid anymore. Some returned. Those who didn't return would possibly never recover and spend the rest of their lives in mental fog.

Then there were the combat-fatigue cases. Some seemed unaware of their surroundings, while others sobbed silently. Others screamed and shouted. The rain, the constant shellings increased the strain beyond that of many young marine's endurance.

Most had serious trouble with their feet. For a period fifteen days, the marine's feet were soaking wet, and their boondockers were caked with sticky mud. Consequently, most men's feet were in bad condition. Their feet were sore, and it hurt to walk or run.

Sore feet caused by prolonged exposure to mud and water was called immersion foot. In World War I they called the same condition trench foot. It was the kind of experience that would make a man grateful for the rest of his life for clean, dry socks.

The almost-constant rain also caused skin on their fingers to develop a shrunken and wrinkled appearance. The nails softened. Sores developed on the knuckles and the back of the hands. Scabs were knocked off against ammunition boxes.

There was little or nothing Thad or the doctors could do to treat these non-combat injuries. Tell a man to keep his feet dry? Avoid the mud?

23

Meanwhile, the Sixth Marine Division was taking their licks and having trouble securing Sugar Loaf Hill. Thad and Plowboy were bailing out their foxhole when word came down. "Stand by. Prepare to move out."

"Thank you, Lord."

"Don't go thanking the Lord too soon, Bubba," said the NCO that had delivered the word. It was the Mouse.

"You done got yourself promoted."

"Good work does not go unrewarded. You might want to keep that in mind. The battalion is moving over to Sugar Loaf to help out the Sixth who are getting their collective butts kicked."

"Aw, c'mon, Mouse. Tell me you're shittin' me."

"Kid you not. Get off your butts and get moving."

Plowboy told him, "I heard what happens when a little guy gets a taste of authority. Look at Napoleon. He was only about four feet tall. A little taller than you."

"Was not. I'm taller than him. Move."

After squaring away their gear as much as possible, they were issued ammunition, water, and rations. They formed up, wheeled right, and began trudging through the mud toward Sugar Loaf

Hill. There wasn't the usual griping and complaining. By now the marines had become hardened and accustomed to misery. They no longer cared.

When they were still several hundred yards from the base of the hill, they came under fire, mostly mortars, machine guns, and rifle fire. They dug in, if only temporarily, and were ordered to move out. They'd covered perhaps four or five hundred yards when the shelling became even more intense. Thad and Plowboy dug in one more time.

The shelling increased in volume, and now the explosions were more violent. Japanese artillery and mortars had found the range. One of the new guys, Thad didn't know his name, was caught out in the open during the barrage. He ran toward the protection of a bomb crater. Ten yards at most. Might as well have been a hundred-yard dash or a country mile. He was almost laughing at himself when he didn't make it. The tremendous explosion made his left leg feel like it was self destructing from its effort to make the one stride that it failed to accomplish. Then, rolling in the mud, he slid down the slope of the crater. He lay in the bottom of it, in a pool of water, while machine gun rounds passed fiercely over him. He looked up the mud slope of the crater and noticed streaks of red along the path where he had slid down the bank. And outside of the crater was the dead part of a marine. A boot with a leg in it. The calf was mildly athletic, perfectly formed but for the angry tear at the top from the explosion. He looked down at his left leg. Most of it was gone.

Thad shouted to Plowboy, "What happened to the new guy?"
Plowboy shouted back, pointing, "He's out there."
"Is he dead?"
"He's in a crater. He was alive a minute ago. I think he's hit."
"Where's the crater?"
Pointing with his rifle, "Just the other side of that one."

Thad grabbed his pouches, and crawled toward the crater, then made a running dive in front of it, and slid down into the hole with the replacement. There was a pool of water at the bottom. The water was brown from the mud, and streaked with large amounts of blood.

"What's your name?"

"Brashear."

"How long you been here, Brashear?"

"Just a few minutes."

"No. How long you been with the company?"

"Three days, I think."

Thad examined the leg, which Brashear had managed to tie off with his belt. Thad pulled the belt tighter cutting off most of the blood flow. "Damn, Brashear, you're a tough sumbitch, aren't you?" but Brashear didn't hear him.

He lay next to baby-faced marine and slapped him in the face.

He turned toward Thad and smiled just a bit, coming out of shock again. He had been drifting in and out of consciousness since tying himself off. Thad turned him around, placing his head at the bottom of the crater, near the pool of water, to lessen the bleeding and to bring him out of shock.

Brashear noticed the blood streak and the deep stains in the water. He smiled again at Thad. He smiled back while trying to determine if it was safe to give him a shot of morphine. He decided to wait.

"You're going to be okay, man."

"Brashear shook his head side to side, His helmet was gone.

"You hit anywhere else? How'd it happen?"

"It doesn't matter. We're all going to die."

"Nah. We're the good guys." He decided it was safe to medicate him, and they waited for the stretcher bearers.

That night more of the same. No frontal attacks. No banzai

charges. Rain, mud, mortars, artillery, and star shells, and the misery. The misery had become a constant, just as the rain had.

During a lull in the bombardment, Plowboy asked Thad, "What do you think this stinking hill is worth in American lives? Or Japanese lives?"

"If the powers that be would look at it like that, maybe there wouldn't be anymore wars. What do you think?"

Thad said, "It's not worth one American life. Not one. I don't know about the Japanese. They seem to want to die."

After considering this, Plowboy said, "You ever wanted to die, Doc?"

"I don't think so, but there were times when I thought I'd like to be wounded so I could get off this island. But then I remember what my mother used to tell me. Be careful what you wish for. A wound could be a broken leg. Or an explosion that takes off both legs. Then I just pray for this war to be over soon. I think that's about all any of us can do."

Thad asked, "What are you going to do when you get out?"

"Hell, I don't know. Haven't really given it a lot of thought. I was raised on a dairy farm, and those early-morning milkings get old. Them cows don't care if it's Sunday, Christmas, or your birthday. They gotta be milked. I guess maybe finish high school first, and think about college. None of my folks have ever been to college, and we got the opportunity. Be a shame to pass it up. Don't know what I'd study though. Maybe Animal Husbandry, as long as it don't have nothing to do with milking cows. How about you Doc? You gonna' be a doctor?"

"I doubt it. I've seen enough pain and suffering to last me two lifetimes."

With the dawn came the rains and one more time the order to move out. They hadn't advanced more than a hundred yards when the mortar and artillery fire stopped them. A violent explosion, a belch of smoke and dust, and a man running in front of Thad did a full flip in the air. His rifle spun away like a baton, and he landed where he had stood only a half second before, but now he was a scorched, decapitated ash heap, that once again reminded Thad how very close he stayed to death. Another explosion. One moment the man was there. The next he disappeared.

Thad watched another marine, one of the replacements, half jogging when the earth behind him erupted. He sailed forward, landed on his back, and when he finally opened his eyes, Thad was near him, yanking out a handful of battle dressings.

The marine noticed the ooze that covered his arms. He felt it in his hair and along his neck and on the back of his legs and shoulder. He tried to sit, and finally rolled over on his stomach. He told Thad, "Gimme a shot of morphine, Doc. They got me."

Thad dressed as many of the wounds as he could until he ran out of bandages, and told Plowboy to go find another corpsman and bring back more battle dressings, while Thad administered a dose of the morphine.

By the time Plowboy returned, the marine was laughing.

Thad finished his work and told him that the stretcher bearers would take him out of here.

After digging in word finally came down that while Sugar Loaf wasn't secure, the Sixth was making progress, and the battalion was to retrace its steps and return to their position in Wana Draw. That was, providing the Japs hadn't taken it over during their absence.

They hadn't. *I don't guess they want it. If they don't want it, why should we? Mine not to reason why.*

Toward the end of May, the rain began to slacken, and rumors spread that the marines would go on attack soon. They heard that the Japanese had withdrawn from their main defensive position on Shuri Heights, but they had left a strong rear guard to fight to the death, so the marines could expect no signs of weakness. But Shuri was where the fire was coming from that had been destroying the battalion piece by piece, man by man. "Maybe they'll take their artillery and mortars with them, and we can catch a break. Is that too much to ask?"

Apparently not. The enemy had withdrawn guns and troops from Shuri to the extent that the shelling of their area had all but stopped, but the drizzling rain remained. Almost out on his feet with fatigue, Thad decided to take advantage of the quiet. He unfolded an unused stretcher, set it on some boards and lay down, covered himself with his poncho. It was the first time in two months that he was able to lie down on anything but hard ground or mud. The canvas stretcher felt like a feather bed, and he soon fell into a deep sleep.

After a while he felt himself being lifted upward. *"Is this it? Am I on my way to meet my maker?"* He awoke with a jerk and realized that someone had picked up the stretcher. He threw off the poncho, jumped off the stretcher and spun around and saw two marines looking at him in utter astonishment.

The two strangers were graves-registration men. They had picked up the stretcher thinking he was just another poncho-covered corpse. They grinned when they realized what had happened, but Rat and Roy Boy were laughing like a couple of fools, all the while denying they had anything to do with it.

On 28 May dawn broke without rain, and they prepared to attack later in the morning. At mid-morning they attacked against long-range mortar and machine-gun fire. The opposition was light, and the sun was shining. Life was good. They actually advanced several hundred yards that day, quite an accomplishment in that sector.

Moving through the mud was still difficult, but they were glad to finally get out of the stinking, half-flooded garbage pit around Half Moon. That night they learned that they would continue the attack the next day by moving directly against the Shuri Ridge.

The next morning they attacked and reached the ruins of Shuri Castle. Although the place was in ruins, Thad could see that the area had been impressive and picturesque before its destruction by the U.S. bombardment. Shuri Castle itself was a mess, and it was hard to tell about its former appearance. It had been an ancient stone building, surrounded by a moat and what appeared to have been terraces and gardens. It was once a pretty place. Now it was rubble.

They dug in that night with the knowledge that even though they had at last taken Shuri Ridge, there were still strongly entrenched Japanese still in Wana Draw, but they remained quiet during the night.

The marines attacked again the next day and got shelled badly. They moved into a muddy, slippery ridge and were told to dig in along the crest. The weather turned bad again, and it started raining. Lieutenant Pond ordered them to dig two-man foxholes five yards apart along the crest of the ridge.

The ridge was about a hundred feet high and steep. Japanese packs, helmets, and other gear lay scattered along the crest. From the looks of the place it must have been shelled heavily for a long time. The air was foul with the odor of rotting flesh. The ridge was a putrid place, just like Half Moon Hill.

Thad and Shotgun began digging their foxhole, men on both sides of them cursing the stench and the mud. Thad began moving the heavy, sticky clay mud with his entrenching tool to shape out the extent of the foxhole before digging deeper. Each shovel full had to be knocked off the shovel, because it stuck like glue. Thad was thoroughly exhausted and thought his strength wouldn't last from one sticky shovelful to the next.

Shotgun took over. Kneeling in the mud, he had dug the hole no more than six or eight inches deep when the odor of rotting flesh got worse. There was nothing to do but keep digging, so he closed his mouth and inhaled with short, shallow breaths. Another shovelful of soil out of the hole released a mass of maggots. "It's all yours, Doc."

Thad found an NCO and showed him what they were uncovering and told him they had to dig somewhere else. "You heard the man. Five yards apart. Keep digging."

Disgusted, he drove the little shovel into the soil, scooped out the maggots and threw them down the front of the ridge. The next stroke of the shovel unearthed buttons and scraps of cloth from a Japanese army jacket buried in the mud—and another mass of maggots. Keep digging. With the next thrust, metal hit the breastbone of a rotting Japanese corpse. He gagged as the metal scraped a clean track through the mud along the dirty whitish bone and cartilage with ribs attached. The odor overwhelmed him as he rocked back on his heels.

Choking and gagging, he yelled in desperation, "I can't dig here. There's a dead Jap in here."

The NCO came back, "Five yards apart. Get with it."

"How the hell can I dig a foxhole with a dead Jap in it?"

Just then, Sergeant Bradley came along and said, "What's the matter, Doc?"

He pointed to the partially exhumed corpse. The sergeant immediately told the NCO to have him dig off to the side, away from the rotting remains. He thanked Sergeant Bradley and glared at the NCO. He didn't know how he managed to keep from vomiting during this vile experience.

As soon as they had a proper foxhole dug off to the side of their first attempt, with several shovels full of dirt thrown into that excavation, Thad and Shotgun began squaring away their gear for the coming night. There was some small-arms fire, but other than that, it was pretty quiet. Sergeant Bradley was down at the foot of the ridge behind them with a map in his hand. He called for the NCOs to come down for a critique and a briefing on the next day's attack.

Rat took one step off the ridge, slipped, and fell. He slid on his belly all the way to the bottom, like a kid going down one of those slides at the neighborhood swimming pool. He was, of course, muddy from the slide, but that was the least of it. White, fat maggots fell off his cartridge belt, pockets and folds of his dungaree jacket and trousers. Roy Boy, who had made it down without falling, picked up a stick, handed Rat another, and together they began scraping the nasty, repulsive little larvae off his dungarees.

He wasn't ordered to hold this little critique, but Sergeant Bradley wanted his men to know what was going on. He showed them a map of the battlefield and explained recent events and future attack plans. The gesture was appreciated, because usually orders were given, and the men rarely knew what was going on. They were told to go, and they went. The sergeant asked if there were any questions. A few were asked, and he answered. Then they slowly climbed back up the filthy ridge after he dismissed them.

That night the rains came down in torrents, one terrific deluge, the worst they had seen. The wind blew, the rain stung their faces. Visibility was limited to the point where they couldn't see the men in foxholes on either side of them. Most were thinking, *What a terrible night to grapple with Japanese infiltrators.*

There was considerable machine-gun fire, bursts of rifle fire and grenade explosions, but their immediate area was relatively quiet. The next morning the realized why they weren't molested by the enemy. The Japanese simply couldn't crawl up the slick surface.

24

They pushed past Shuri over some muddy hills in the Army's zone of action and came across a group of about twenty Japanese prisoners. Each man was stripped except for a little g-string-like garment. They stood barefooted alongside the trail. Several dirty and battle-weary Army infantrymen guarded them. The captured enemy had been ordered off the trail by an interpreter so the marines could pass.

They moved rapidly through open country in a torrential rain, finally entering a village of houses and several smaller huts. All of the dwellings had to be checked. While searching one of the huts, Thad came across an old Okinawan woman seated on the floor just inside the doorway. Taking no chances, with his carbine he motioned for her to get up. She remained on the floor and said, "No Nippon." Obviously in pain, she opened her ragged blue kimono and pointed to a wound on the lower left side of her abdomen. It was an old wound, probably caused by shell or bomb fragments. A large area around the scabbed over gash was discolored and terribly infected with gangrene. Thad knew that such a severe infection was always fatal.

The old woman closed her kimono, and reached up and took

the muzzle of his carbine and directed it between her eyes. Then she released the weapon's barrel and motioned for him to pull the trigger. He laid the weapon on the ground, shook his head, "No." Reached into his pouch, removed sulfa and a bandage, motioned for her to open her kimono. He applied the sulfa and bandage, knowing it was too little, too late. He opened a can of fruit cocktail he had been saving, handed it to the woman, nodded to her, picked up his carbine, and left her sitting there holding the can of fruit cocktail in her lap.

That was Thad's first encounter with any Okinawan civilian. He wondered how many innocents had been killed, wounded, maimed by the war. How many dead from the thunderous American pre-invasion shelling? How many from American artillery and mortars? How many from Japanese munitions? He thought, surely thousands. They had been living peacefully on their once-beautiful island, then these American marines and soldiers came and took that away, destroyed their homes, their lives. Did they hate the Americans? Probably. Who could blame them? When they finally left then what?

They moved out of the village and dug in with the ruins of the Okinawan houses behind them and a broad open valley to their front as far as they could see. The rain had ended, and Thad removed his soaked, muddy boondockers for the first time in two weeks. As he pulled off his slimy, stinking socks pieces of flesh fell off the soles of his feet. He threw the socks off to the side and shoveled dirt over them like he was covering a corpse. He had buried his socks. *Shouldn't someone be playing taps? You're cracking, Hayes. Might be time for you to think of another career.*

He washed his feet in his helmet. Propped them up on an ammo box alongside his boondockers to let the sun shine on them. It felt good. One of life's little pleasures. While it felt good, his feet were extremely sore. The soles were red and raw, almost to the point of bleeding. But after drying them in the sun and putting on clean socks and dry boondockers, they felt better.

Between patrols they began to get rested and dried out. The battle seemed to be winding down. They had air drops of supplies, food, water, and ammunition. During the day they could build fires and heat rations. Not quite stateside duty, but close enough.

On the morning of 4 June, Gunny Mancillas asked for two volunteers to carry a message to the coast regarding supplies. "Doc, you and Joe Louis Boyd." Their instructions were straightforward: "Stay on the main east-west road all the way to the beach and back." They were told whom to contact and what to ask for. Then they were warned against screwing around and cautioned about the possibility of bypassed enemy.

They started off in high spirits. They were getting a welcome break from the everyday. They had gotten cleaned up by then. Their dungarees had been washed, leggings, and boondockers dry and scraped clean of mud. They carried the usual two canteens of water, a couple of chocolate bars to sustain them for several hours, and their weapons. Thad had his carbine and .45, Joe Louis Boyd had his M-1. The weather had dried out, and it was an ideal day for a little harmless diversion from the patrols they had been making.

After they moved out of their battalion area and onto the road, they saw no one. The only sounds were the sounds of their own voices, the crunching of their boondockers on the road, the silent world that characterized the aftermath of war.

They encountered numerous enemy corpses, which they always passed on the windward side. They saw no marine dead, but a bloody dungaree jacket here, a torn boondocker there, a helmet ripped by bullets and bloody battle dressings, were reminders of the fate of their former owners.

They entered the outskirts of a town. All of the buildings were badly damaged, but some were still standing. One was a little store. In the street in front of the store lay a corpse clad in a blue kimono, probably the proprietor of the little store. Someone had placed a broken door over the pathetic little body. A grim reminder. They passed a burned-out bus station with the ticket booth still standing. They could hear the distant rumblings of battle as the Sixth Marine Division was hopefully ridding the island of any remaining enemy.

They continued through the ruins toward the beach without incident, when an amtrac came rattling toward them. The driver was the first living soul that they had seen. They waved him down, and it turned out he was expecting them at the beach, and had started along the road hoping to locate them. They gave the driver the information that the gunny had told them to deliver. The amtrac spun around and headed back toward the beach. With their mission completed, they started back along the road toward the ruins.

They passed the little store and the dead Okinawan woman covered by the door and approached the bus station. A gentle breeze was blowing. Only the clanking of a piece of loose tin on the ruined bus station broke the silence. Since they had saved time by meeting the amtrac, Thad and Joe Louis Boyd decided to explore the bus station and eat their rations there. Just another peaceful summer afternoon.

The long burst of a Japanese machine gun, bullets zipping by, chest high sent them scrambling for cover. They dove behind the concrete ticket booth and lay on the rubble, breathing hard.

"Damn, that was close, Doc!"

"Too damned close! The guy had his elevation zeroed in perfectly, but he led us too much."

The bullets ricocheted and whined around inside the burned-out bus station. They heard the tinkle of glass as the slugs broke windows among the burned-out busses.

"Where the hell is he?" asked Joe Louis Boyd.

"I don't know, but he's probably a couple hundred yards away from the sound of the gun."

They lay motionless for a moment, the silence broken only by clanking of the tin in the breeze. Cautiously, Thad peered out from behind the base of the ticket booth. Another burst of slugs narrowly missed his head and went clattering through the building after striking the concrete alongside them.

"He's got us zeroed in for sure."

The ticket booth was surrounded by an open expanse of concrete in all directions. The gunner had them pinned down. Joe Louis Boyd peeped around his side of the ticket booth and got the same reception as Thad. The enemy machine gunner then fired a long burst across the top of the concrete portion of the booth, shattering what was left of the window. By now, they were sure that the gunner was on the opposite side of a railroad embankment.

"Why don't you go get him, Joe? I'll wait here."

"In your dreams, white boy. Maybe we can get back among them busses and out of sight and then slip out the rear of the building." He moved slightly to one side to look behind them, and another burst of fire blew that plan all to hell.

"I guess we'll have to wait till dark and then slip out of here," Thad said.

"You're right. We sure as hell ain't going to get out of here during the daylight. He's got us pinned down tighter than Dick's hat band."

"Dick's hat band? Where the hell did that come from?"

"Don't have time nor the inclination to educate you now. What are we going to do?"

"Wait."

The minutes grew into hours as time dragged by while they kept a lookout in all directions in case other Japanese might slip in behind them.

Toward late afternoon they heard the burst of M-1 rifle fire over in the direction where the enemy gunner was located. After a few minutes, Joe Louis Boyd said, "Take a look, Doc. See if it's safe."

"You first."

"No. You first, " and they both laughed.

After a few minutes, here comes Roy Boy, Rat, and Boudreau, strolling in.

"Look out for that Jap Machine gunner!"

A grinning Rat held up the machine gun and said, "The gunny figured you'd run into trouble when you didn't come back and sent us out to look for you."

They continued their patrols, but the day soon came with the inevitable order, "Square away your gear. We're moving out again."

The weather had turned dry and warm as they moved south. The farther they proceeded, the louder the sound of firing became. Along with the sounds, came the old feelings of dread about one's own chances of survival.

They were approaching another ridge, Kunishi Ridge. They plodded along the sides of a dusty road, next to tanks and amtracs moving forward and a steady stream of ambulance jeeps returning loaded with the human wreckage of the battle of Kunishi Ridge.

That afternoon the company deployed along a row of trees and bushes. They saw and heard the heavy firing on Kunishi Ridge across the open ground ahead of them. Nearby was a picturesque bridge that had remained intact over a high stream bank.

Thad, Rat, and Shotgun went to look at the bridge before dark. They walked down to the stream where the water ran crystal clear and made a gurgling sound over a pebbly bottom. Ferns grew from the overhanging mossy banks and between rocks on both sides. It was a beautiful place, cool and peaceful, so out of context with the nearby hell close above it.

The next morning as they moved up toward the ridge they heard sirens for the first time. Roy Boy said, "What the hell is that?"

Rat told him it was the Okinawa Police Department coming to arrest them for fucking up their country. They were told that the Army had put sirens on their tanks for the psychological effect it might have on the Japs. To Thad, the sirens just made the whole bloody struggle more bizarre and unnerving. The Japanese didn't surrender in the face of flamethrowers, artillery, bombs, or anything else, so he couldn't understand how harmless sirens would bother them. They got tired of hearing them wailing, against the explosions and the constant rattle of small arms fire.

That night, they heard that they would attack the next morning to capture the remainder of Kunishi Ridge. One more time. *Into the valley of death rode the six hundred.*

They learned that they would move out well before daylight and deploy for the attack, because they had to move across a wide-open area to get to the ridge. Moving in the darkness was something the marines didn't like. They were strong in their belief that only the Japanese or damned fools moved around at night, but moving up under the cover of darkness was the only way to approach the ridge.

They moved slowly and cautiously, while up ahead they could see shells exploding on and around the ridge. They heard rifle fire, the rattling of machine guns, and the banging of grenades. They knew that this was probably the last big fight before the Japanese were wiped out, and they would fight to the very last man. While Thad plodded along through the darkness his heart was pounding, and his throat was dry, and near-panic seized him. Having made it that far in the war, he knew his luck would run out. He prayed that when he got hit it wouldn't result in death or maiming. He wanted to turn and run away.

They moved up onto the ridge, and the fighting was close, with the Japanese on the reverse slope. The Eleventh Marines 105 artillery was firing over the ridge as they moved into position in the dark. A shell exploded short in the company line. The company CP alerted the forward observer that they had received short rounds. Another 105 round went off with a terrible explosion.

The artillery was firing across Kunishi Ridge into and around the town of Kunishi to prevent the enemy from moving more troops onto the ridge. But each time they shot, it seemed that one of the guns fired its shells in a pattern right along the company's line.

"Corpsman!" someone yelled.

Thad rushed to the injured man. It was Sergeant Bradley. He'd been hit by shrapnel from one of the short rounds. When Thad reached him the sergeant sat up and said, "They got me. The Japs couldn't get me. My own artillery got me. War's hell, ain't it, Doc?"

His right arm was bleeding badly. It was crooked and was surely broken.

"Where else you hit besides your arm?"

"My left leg, I think."

Thad cut his pant leg. The wound seemed to be superficial, ripping away skin and about a quarter inch of meat.

He dressed the wounds, fashioned a sling for the broken arm, and asked him if he needed morphine.

"Hell no! I'm going back to the Eleventh Marines and find the sonofabitch that shot me and kick his ass."

"A one-armed sergeant kicking a cannon-cocker's ass?"

"No contest, Doc. No contest."

Thad believed him and made arrangements to get him transported back to the rear.

Snipers were all over the ridge and almost impossible to locate. Men began getting shot one right after another, and stretcher teams kept on the run. The casualties were brought down to the base of the ridge to the point where tanks could back in out of the view of the snipers on the ridge. Thad and other corpsmen treated the wounded and tied them onto stretchers and then tied the stretchers onto the rear deck of the tanks. Then the tanks took off in a cloud of dust toward the aid station. As many men as possible fired along the ridge to pin down the snipers so they couldn't shoot the wounded on the tanks.

Thad helped load Sergeant Bradley onto one of the tanks. He told the sergeant the tank driver was going to drop him off at the Eleventh Marines so he could get on with his ass kicking.

The sergeant was hurting by now, and all he could do was smile. And say, "Maybe later."

From Thad's position on the ridge he watched a stretcher team make its way up the ridge to bring down a casualty. Suddenly, four or five mortar rounds exploded in quick succession near the team, wounding three of the four bearers. They helped each other back down the ridge, and another stretcher team started up to get the casualty. To avoid the enemy mortar observer, they moved up a slightly different route. They got up the ridge and found the casualty lying above a sheer coral ledge, about five feet high. The marine told the team that he couldn't move much because he had been shot in both feet. He couldn't lower himself down off the ridge. "You guys be careful. The guy that shot me twice is still hiding right over there in those rocks." He motioned toward a pile of boulders not more than twenty feet away.

One of the bearers shouted that they needed help. Roy Boy, who happened to be nearby, made his way to them and asked what they needed. They explained the situation. Roy Boy studied the rocks where the sniper was hiding and told the team to sit tight.

He back tracked for twenty or thirty yards and began climbing the rocks. He was out of sight for several minutes from the stretcher team, and they had begun to wonder if he had just taken off and left them to solve their own problem.

Roy Boy had climbed the boulders until he was directly above the cave where the fire was coming from. He removed a grenade, pulled the pin, and tossed it in. It exploded. Black smoke belched out of the hole, then silence. He dropped down in front of the cave, and with a Tommy gun he had just recently picked up, sprayed the cave's interior, entered it, and there he was. The Jap machine gunner, or what was left of him. Roy Boy then took the machine gun and threw it down off the ridge, made his way down to the wounded marine, and told the stretcher bearers, "He's all yours."

The casualty thanked him, and Roy Boy told him to forget it. "You'd have done the same for me."

Toward afternoon several of the men were resting among the rocks near the crest of the ridge. Thad, Rat, Boudreau, and a boy named James something had been passing ammunition and water up to some men just below the crest. A Japanese machine gun still covered the crest there, and no one dared raise his head. Bullets snapped over the crest, whined, banged, and ricocheted wildly among the rocks. James, who had been with the company on Peleliu, seemed unusually quiet and moody during the past hour, but Thad figured he was just as weary with fatigue and fear as the rest of them. But he started babbling incoherently. He grabbed his rifle and shouted, "Those slant-eyed, yellow bastards have killed enough of my friends! I'm going after 'em!" He jumped up and started for the crest of the ridge.

Thad yelled, "Stop!" and grabbed at his trouser leg. He pulled away. Rat also grabbed at the frantic man's legs, but missed. He managed to clutch the toe of one boondocker and gave a jerk. That threw the man off balance, and he sprawled on his back, bawling like a baby. The front of his trousers were wet where he had urinated when he lost control of himself. They tried to calm him while making sure he didn't get back on his feet. "Take it easy, James. We'll get you out of here."

Finally, Thad managed to take the sobbing, trembling man back to the aid station.

"He's a good marine. Just had all he can take. That's all. Just had all he can take."

They had just seen a brave man crack up completely, even to the point of losing his desire to live.

On the afternoon of 18 June the company was relieved on Kunishi Ridge, Thad asked Lieutenant Pond how many men they had lost in the fighting. He told him they had lost forty-nine enlisted men and one officer, half their number of the previous day. Almost all of the newly arrived replacements were among the casualties. Now the company became a mere remnant, twenty-one percent of its normal strength of 235 men. They had been on Kunishi Ridge for less than twenty-four hours.

The fight for Kunishi Ridge, from 11-18 June, cost the First Marine Division 1,150 casualties. The fight marked the end of organized Japanese resistance on Okinawa.

25

The company came down off Kunishi Ridge late in the day on 18 June and started winding their way south. They moved into a valley at five-pace intervals, one file on each side of the road. An amtrac came clattering slowly along, headed toward the front further south, when someone yelled, "Disperse!"

Everyone scattered, most jumping into a shallow ditch. The first enemy antitank shell passed over the top of the amtrac, but the second scored a direct hit on the left side. The machine jolted to a stop and started smoking. The driver tried to re-start the engine as two more shells slammed into the side of the disabled amtrac. The two marines in the cab jumped out and into the ditch next to Thad.

"What kind of cargo you carrying?"

"We got a full unit of fire for a rifle company. Ammunition, grenades, mortar ammo—the works. When that fire reach reaches the ammunition, and she blows, it's going to be one helluva fireworks display."

The driver crawled off down the ditch to find a radio operator to report that his load of ammunition couldn't get through.

Just then came a flash accompanied by a loud explosion and terrific concussion as the amtrac blew up.

Four or five Marine tanks were parked close together in the valley downhill from them about a hundred yards away. They swung their 75s around and opened up on the Jap 47-mm gun battery that had knocked out the amtrac, which was now firing on the tanks. It was a good, old-fashioned shoot out.

The Japanese were remarkably accurate. Several of their tracer-like armor-piercing shells could be seen hitting the turrets of the tanks and ricocheting off into the air. After a few minutes of this duel, the Marine tanks won, the Japanese guns were knocked out, and everything got quiet. The tanks sustained only minor damage. The marines went back onto the road and resumed their march south.

They used loudspeakers, captured Japanese soldiers, and Okinawan civilians to persuade the remaining enemy to surrender. One sergeant and a Japanese lieutenant who had graduated from a Ivy League college and spoke perfect English gave themselves up. Just after they surrendered and were surrounded by eight or ten marines, a sniper opened fire on them. The marines hit the ditch while the Japanese officer and sergeant stood in the middle of the road with bullets kicking up dirt all around them. The sniper obviously was trying to kill them because they had surrendered. An NCO yelled at them to take cover. The enemy officer grinned and spoke to his sergeant. They finally walked over and got down as ordered.

They passed a cave sheltering a 105-mm howitzer crew. A lieutenant from another company jumped in front of the cave and in Japanese said, "Come out. I will not harm you." Then he fired a complete twenty round magazine from his submachine gun into the cave. Thad just shook his head and moved on.

The battalion was the first to reach the end of the island. It was a beautiful sight even though there were still snipers around. They stood on a high hill above the sea. They could see Army troops advancing toward them flushing out enemy soldiers, singly and in small groups. The night of 20 June they made a defensive line on the high ground overlooking the sea.

That night turned into a long series of shooting scrapes. Japs prowled all over the place. They could hear the enemy soldiers' hobnailed boots pounding on the road. Other Japanese swam or walked along in the sea just offshore. They could be seen beneath the flares. A line of marines behind a stone wall were picking them off all night long.

Just before daylight, they heard a couple of enemy grenades explode. Japanese yelled and shouted where the gunny and other NCOs were taking shelter in a gun emplacement across the road. Shots rang out, then shouts and cursing.

"Corpsman!" Then silence.

Thad ran toward the gun emplacement where the call for help had come from. When he got there another corpsman was bandaging one of the NCOs. Two of them had been wounded when two enemy officers crept up the steep slope, threw grenades into the gun emplacement, and jumped in swinging their samurai swords. The gunny had parried the blow with his carbine, and then shot the Japanese officer who fell backwards down the slope. The saber blow had severed a finger and sliced through the carbine stock to the metal barrel.

The second Japanese officer lay dead on his back. He was in full-dress uniform with white gloves, shiny leather leggings, Sam Browne belt, and campaign ribbons on his chest. Nothing remained of his head from the nose up, just a mass of crushed skull, brains, and bloody pulp. A grimy marine with a dazed expression stood over the Japanese. With a foot planted firmly on the ground on each side of the enemy officer's body, the marine held his rifle by the forestock with both hands and slowly and mechanically moved it up and down like a plunger. Thad winced each time it came down with a sickening thud into the gory mass. Brains and blood were spattered all over the marine's rifle, boondockers and canvas leggings.

The poor guy was obviously in a complete state of shock. One of his buddies gently took his arm and said, "Let's get you out of here, Willie." He responded like a sleepwalker as he was led off with the wounded, who were by then on stretchers.

Meanwhile, Gunny Mancillas clutched the saber in his other hand. "I'm going to keep this thing for a souvenir."

Thad said, "Good idea, but we better get you home before the Japs decide to take another piece out of your hide. Half of your ear, and now a finger."

As Thad bandaged what was left of the finger, Gunny looked at it and said. "Won't be able to give the one finger salute with that hand will I?"

"No, but you can still hold up your hand and say, 'We're number one. Or one and a half."

They dragged the battered enemy officer to the edge of the emplacement and rolled him down the hill. Thad thought, *This is the type of incident that should be witnessed by anyone who has any delusions about the glory of war. We're no more than barbarians rather than civilized men.*

Later in the day of 21 June, 1945, they learned that the high command had declared the island secured. They each received two fresh oranges with the compliments of Admiral Nimitz. Thad couldn't believe that Okinawa had finally ended. He was tempted to relax and think that they would board ship immediately for rest and rehabilitation in Hawaii. However he was skeptical, and his intuition proved accurate. Mopping up was the grim news.

"You people will mop up the area for any Japs still holding out.

You will bury all enemy dead. You will salvage U.S. and enemy equipment. All brass above .50 caliber in size will be collected and placed in neat piles. Stand by to move out."

To the battle-weary troops, exhausted after an eighty-two-day campaign, mopping up was the final indignation. It was nerve wracking business. The enemy they had encountered were the toughest of the diehards. The marines had survived the battle against the law of averages. They were nervous and jittery. A man could survive Tarawa, Peleliu, and Okinawa only to be shot by some fanatical, bypassed Japanese holed up in a cave. It was hard to accept the order. But they did—grimly. Burying enemy dead and collecting brass and equipment on the battlefield was the last straw to their sagging morale.

Fighting was their duty. Their job, but burying enemy dead and cleaning up the battlefield wasn't for infantry troops, as they saw it. They complained and griped bitterly. They had fought and won. They were infuriated and frustrated. For the first time, Thad saw several of his veteran comrades flatly refuse to obey an order. They would be punished for insubordination.

They dragged themselves back to the skirmish line and cursed every enemy dead they had to bury. (They just spaded dirt over them with their entrenching shovels.) They cursed every cartridge case "above .50 caliber in size they collected to "place in neat piles." Flame-throwing tanks were particularly effective in burning out troublesome Japanese in caves. Fortunately they had few casualties.

In a few days they assembled in an open field and fell out to await further orders. The weather was hot. They all took of their packs and sat on their helmets. After a short wait, Thad, Boudreau, and five or six others were told to get their gear and follow an NCO to waiting trucks. They were to go north to a site where the division would make a tent camp after the mop-up in the south was completed.

They were apprehensive about leaving the company, but it turned out to be good duty. The land around their future campsite was undamaged. They unloaded company gear from the truck. They had five-gallon cans of water and plenty of K rations.

Their little guard detail spent several quiet, carefree days basking in the sun by day and mounting one sentry guard duty at night. They were like boys on a camp out. The fear and terror were behind them.

The battalion came north a few days later. All hands went to work in earnest to complete the tent camp. Tents were set up, drainage ditches were dug, folding cots and bed rolls were brought to them, and a canvas-roofed mess hall was built. Every day old friends returned from the hospitals, some hale and hearty but others showing the effects of only partial recovery from severe wounds. To their disgust, rumors of rehabilitation in Hawaii faded, but knowing that the long Okinawa ordeal was over at last was indescribable.

Among those returning from the hospital was Sergeant Bradley, appearing none the worse for wear, other than the cast on his right arm. When asked if he ever caught up with that damn cannon cocker that shot him, he said, "Every Eleventh Marine I talked to is in denial, claiming they know nothing about the short rounds they put on us that night. I'll find him, though. As long as he doesn't muster out before I do, I'll find him."

Thad didn't doubt him. After all, he was Superman.

Very few familiar faces were left. Only twenty-six of the Tarawa and Peleliu veterans who landed with the company on 1 April remained. Total American casualties were 7,613 killed and missing and 31,807 wounded in action. marines and attached naval personnel suffered casualties of 20,020 killed, wounded and missing.

Japanese casualty figures are hazy; however, 107,539 enemy dead were counted on Okinawa. Approximately 10,000 enemy troops surrendered, and about 20,000 were either sealed in caves or buried by the Japanese themselves. Unfortunately, approximately 42,000 Okinawan civilians, caught between two opposing armies, perished from artillery fire and bombing.

As they finished building their tent camp, they began trying to unwind from the grueling campaign. Ugly rumors circulated that they would hit Japan next, with an expected casualty figure of one million Americans. No one wanted to talk about that.

On 8 August, they heard that the first atomic bomb had been dropped on Japan. Reports abounded for a week about a possible surrender. Then on 15 August 1945 the war ended.

They received the news with quiet disbelief coupled with an indescribable sense of relief. They thought the Japanese would never surrender. Many refused to believe it. Sitting around in silence they remembered their dead. So many dead. So many maimed. So many bright futures gone. So many dreams lost in the madness. Except for a few widely scattered shouts of joy, the survivors sat hollow eyed and silent, trying to comprehend a world without war.

In September the First Marine Division went to North China on occupation duty. After four-and-a-half months there, Thad rotated stateside. One of America's finest and most famous elite fighting divisions had been Thad's home during a period of the most extreme adversity. It was time to say goodbye to old buddies. Severing the ties formed in three campaigns was painful. They had forged a bond that time would never erase. They were brothers.

War is a brutish terrible waste. Combat leaves an indelible mark on those who are forced to endure it. The only redeeming factors are comrades' incredible bravery and their devotion to each other. Marine Corps' training taught them to kill efficiently and to try to survive. But it also taught them loyalty to each other and love. That esprit de corps sustained them.

"If the country is good enough to live in, it's good enough to fight for." With privilege goes responsibility.

26
Kamikaze

"Planes rained down from the skies like locusts, crashing and exploding into heaps of twisted metal."

The term itself, "kamikaze," means "divine wind." Its origin traces back to 1281, when a massive typhoon destroyed Kubla Khan's fleet and his opportunity to invade Japan. The decision to launch kamikaze attacks only came in 1944, when Japan's defeat seemed imminent. Hundreds of young Japanese now made the ultimate sacrifice.

The peak in kamikaze attacks came during the period of April-June 1945, at the battle of Okinawa. On April 6, 1945, waves of planes made hundreds of attacks in Operation Kikusuo (floating chrysanthemums). Kamikaze attacks focused at first on Allied destroyers on picket duty and then on the carriers in the middle of the fleet. Suicide attacks by planes or boats at Okinawa sank or put out of action at least thirty U.S. warships and at least three U.S. merchant ships, along with some from other Allied forces. The attacks expended 1,465 planes. Many warships of all classes were damaged, some severely, but no aircraft carriers, battleships, or cruisers were sunk by kamikaze at Okinawa. Most of the ships destroyed were destroyers or smaller vessels, especially those on picket duty, protecting the fleet from the perimeter of the formation.

The establishment of kamikaze forces required recruiting men for the task. This proved easier than the commanders had expected. Qualifications were simple: youth, alertness, and zeal. Flight experience was of minimal importance. "You don't know how to land a plane? No problem, because you aren't going to be landing anyway." Captain Motoharu Okamura commented that there were so many volunteers for suicide missions that he referred to them as a swarm of bees, explaining, "Bees die after they have stung."

When the volunteers arrived for duty in the corps there were twice as many persons as aircraft. After the war, some commanders would express regret for allowing overly eager crews to accompany sorties, squeezing themselves aboard the planes so as to encourage the suicide pilots, and join in the exultation of sinking a large enemy vessel. Many of the kamikaze believed that their death would pay the debt they owed and show the love they had for their families, friends and emperor. So eager were many minimally trained pilots to take part in suicide missions that when their sorties were delayed or aborted, the pilots became deeply despondent. Many of those who were selected for a life-ending mission were described as being extraordinarily blissful immediately before their final sortie.

"When you eliminate all thoughts about life and death, you will be able to totally disregard your earthly life. This will also enable you to concentrate your attention on eradicating the enemy with unwavering determination, meanwhile reinforcing your excellence in flight skills." (A paragraph from a kamikaze pilots' manual.)

Kamikaze-pilot training generally consisted of incredibly strenuous training, coupled with cruel and torturous punishment as a daily routine. One pilot, Irokawa Daikichi, recalled that he "was struck in the face so hard and frequently that his face was no longer recognizable." He also wrote: "I was hit so hard that I could no longer see and fell on the floor. The minute I got up, I was hit again by a club." This brutal "training" was justified by the idea that it would instill a "soldier's fighting spirit." However, daily beatings and corporal punishment eliminated patriotism among many of the pilots.

Pilots were given a manual which detailed how they were supposed to think, prepare, and attack. From this manual, pilots were told to "attain a high level of spiritual training," and to "keep their health in the very best condition." Irokawa probably had a hard time understanding that part. These things, among others, were meant to put the pilot into the mind set in which he would be ready to die.

The pilots' manual also explained how a pilot may turn back if the pilot cannot not locate a target and that "a pilot should not waste his life lightly." However, one pilot who continuously came back to base was shot after his ninth return. Hopefully, not poor Irokawa.

The manual was very detailed in how a pilot should attack. A pilot would dive toward a target and would "aim for a point between the bridge tower and the smoke stacks." Entering a smoke stack was also said to be effective. Pilots were told not to aim at a ships' bridge tower or gun turret but instead to look for elevators or the flight deck to crash into. For horizontal attacks, the pilots were told to "aim at the middle of the vessel, slightly higher than the waterline" or to aim at the entrance to the aircraft hanger, or the bottom of the stack" if the former was too difficult.

The manual told the pilots never to close their eyes. This was because if a pilot closed his eyes he would lower the chances of hitting his target. In the final moments before the crash the pilot was to yell, "Hissatsu!" at the top of his lungs, which roughly translates into "Sink without fail."

The hundreds of pilots that were shot down before reaching any target, before crashing into the ocean, yelled, at the top or his lungs, "Ohshitsu," or the equivalent thereof.

27
McCamey, Texas, 1946

Thad was discharged from the Navy in February, 1946. He had served for the duration of the war, plus six months. He returned to McCamey, appearing to be the same old Thad that had left in 1942, outwardly, at least. But inwardly he was by no means the same old Thad.

Lou Ann had waited and was teaching second grade at McCamey Elementary. She was aware of the changes in Thad and knew that she had to be patient. They avoided the hill overlooking the oil field flares, "Lou Ann's gigantic ballroom." The fires brought back memories, none of them pleasant. He had trouble sleeping, having recurring nightmares. He was sometimes irritable, and any loud, unexpected sound made him jump. He was more often than not depressed. The doctors at the V.A. in Odessa told him that he was suffering from shell shock and battle fatigue, and the only cure was time. They suggested that if he could meet with other veterans, where they could talk about their experiences, perhaps that would help. Thad couldn't see where re-living the war with others could help. What he wanted to do was forget. He'd have to tough it out.

With his mustering out pay, he bought a brand new '46 Ford convertible. He and Lou Ann would take weekend trips to San Antonio, and during her summer vacation they drove to Galveston, checked into the Galvez Hotel, and spent a week doing nothing but lying on the beach and swimming in the Gulf. At night, they would walk across Seawall Boulevard to the Balinese Ballroom, located on a pier well out into the Gulf. There they would do a little gambling, dancing, dining, and they'd enjoy the floorshow. That week it was Jack Benny. In two more weeks it would be Frank Sinatra. They took a quick trip to Houston, where Lou Ann shopped for new clothes for the coming fall, while Thad visited the V.A. there. He got the same diagnosis: battle fatigue. It would eventually go away. It would take time.

He continued to have an occasional nightmare. The depression was still there, but with less frequency. He began to think that he might not be nuts after all. One afternoon while sunning themselves on the beach, Thad seemed to be lost in his own thoughts. These were times when Lou Ann knew not to ask him what he was thinking. He was always thinking about the war. But not this time. He raised up on one elbow, seemed to study Lou Ann for just a moment, and said, "Let's quit sinning, and get married. What do you think?"

"In our swimsuits, or do we have time to change?"

They found a justice of the peace that evening, did the deed, returned to McCamey, and began to plan for the future. Children would come later. She would go back to teaching her second graders while Thad decided what he was going to do. Get a job? Go back to school on the G.I. Bill? *No hurry. Take your time.*

Shell Pipe Line had forgiven him, or perhaps forgotten his previous employment and sudden departure and re-hired him. Since he was now a returning veteran and a responsible married man, they told him he could move into a house at the pumping station outside of town, rent free. Seven other houses were occupied by gaugers and tool pushers.

The job itself hadn't changed, but this time he was not helping welders; he was just doing good old labor. There was lots of shovel work, and no rain to speak of. On those few occasions when it did rain, he was immediately taken back to Okinawa, and seemed to withdraw. The other men on the crew had been told to leave him alone at times like this and ignore him when he jumped at any unexpected loud noise. However, he was accepted, and the men went out of their way to accommodate him in any way possible.

He worked through the winter and spring, and finally told Lou Ann it was time to go back to school. He would go back to A&M and see if there was any way he could improve his grades and somehow get accepted into vet school. He had seen too much human suffering. He had no desire to be a medical doctor. His only interest was in treating animals.

Lou Ann said, "Let's do it," and that fall they took off, one more time, for College Station, only this time, it wasn't with his dad in that old '39 Buick, but with his wife in their red Ford convertible.

He checked in with the registrar, was told he could take those courses that kept him out of vet school the first time, and if he brought them up to As and Bs he would probably be accepted. No problem.

He and Lou Ann moved into Vet Village, apartments for veterans across the street from the campus. In September Thad started classes, and Lou Ann got a job in the Architecture library.

In two semesters, Thad had brought his grades up and was accepted into the School of Veterinary Medicine in August, 1947.

The next four years were spent going to classes, studying at the apartment, or working in the lab. Occasionally he and Lou Ann would go into Bryan for dinner at a nice restaurant or a movie, but only occasionally. Dining out and movies were luxuries that could be barely afforded on his monthly government check. His "battle fatigue" symptoms were slowly disappearing one by one. He had only an occasional nightmare or flashback, and sudden loud noises still made him jump.

In May 1951, he received his diploma and his license to practice veterinary medicine. They returned to McCamey and rented a little one-bedroom bungalow. Lou Ann went back to teaching her second graders, while Thad began his practice with Dr. Sweet. After two years, Dr. Sweet retired, and Thad was the town's only veterinarian. They moved out of their little bungalow, purchased a three-bedroom house, and then came the children, Thad, Jr., and Mary Margaret.

One spring night, Thad, Lou Ann, Thad Jr., and Mary Margaret drove out to Lou Ann's gigantic ballroom. They climbed out of the car and stood on the hill, while the children marveled at the oil field flares. The terrible memories for Thad didn't return. He was back.

Dr. Thadius Hayes, Veterinarian and Mrs. Lou Ann Hayes, school marm. Perfect.

Epilogue

Captain Bartholomew

Captain Harold M. Bartholomew, victim of malaria, was evacuated from Okinawa, and while recovering in the hospital at Hawaii, learned that the island had finally been secured and later that the war was over. Having fully recovered he returned to the States where he was promoted to major and was given command of a battalion at Camp Pendleton, California. In 1951, while leading his battalion in Korea, he was killed by a single rifle bullet at what became known as Heartbreak Ridge.

Lieutenant Pond

Lieutenant Darwin (Duck) Pond remained in the Corps until his retirement as a colonel in 1971. He led a battalion in Korea at the battle of the Chosin Reservoir, where he received the Purple Heart and was awarded a Silver Star. He later commanded a regiment in Vietnam where he received two more purple hearts and Bronze Star. He and his family retired to his birthplace,

Stillwater, Oklahoma, where he presently resides and is often a guest lecturer at Oklahoma State University.

Sergeant Bradley

Sergeant Patrick M. Bradley remained in the Corps. Upon his return to Camp Pendleton, while drinking at a bar in San Clemente, he was making conversation with another marine. He learned that he was a member of the Eleventh Marines. He asked him if he happened to make the Okinawa campaign. "Yes, I did, and it was a bitch." Enough said.

Sergeant Bradley caught him with a right, knocking the poor guy off his stool. "What was that for?"

"Short rounds."

He was promoted to Technical Sergeant, made it through Korea, and while serving in Vietnam, stepped on a mine, taking off both legs. After his discharge, he returned to St, Louis where he worked with the V.A. counseling returning veterans.

Gunny Mancillas

Manuel "Gunny" Mancillas had planned on making the Corps a career, but after the last three campaigns he had had enough. Back in East L.A. he opened a youth club, catering to Hispanic young men, in an attempt to keep them off the streets, out of gangs. He wanted to show them a better way, knowing that there were only three ways: the right way, the wrong way, and the Marine Corps way. Instilling the "Marine Corps way" worked for most of the youths. For others, not so well, which seemed to divide the boys into two groups, the believers and the nonbelievers, which eventually led to a brawl between the two factions with knives, fists, and one .32 automatic. While attempting to break up the fight, it was the .32 that ended the gunny's life. "Ain't this something? Had Japs trying to kill me for four years, and a punk fifteen-year-old with a little bitty pistol shoots me."

Roy Boy

Leroy "Roy Boy" McNabb, who had sworn he'd never pick another peanut, returned to the family farm in Georgia. With a partner, they purchased another five hundred adjoining acres and planted more peanuts. After a few years his partner sold out to Roy Boy and entered politics. He was elected governor and later president of the United States. Roy Boy, alone, became the proprietor of the largest peanut farm in Georgia and was soon producing one-third of the state's peanut crop.

Boudreau and Shotgun

Jean Paul Boudreau and Lewis "Shotgun" Cannon, after their discharge, had decided that they would return to Louisiana and go into business together. They settled in New Iberia on the Bayou Teche. Boudreau told Shotgun that if he was going to live in New Iberia, he would have to pronounce it La Nouvelle Iberia.

Roy Boy told him to "shut the fuck up."

There at New Iberia, or *La Nouvelle Iberia*, depending on which one of the partners was doing the talking, they opened a restaurant, Boudreau's, "Serving the Finest Cajun Cuisine. Open 10 A.M. to midnight." Immediately next door to the restaurant was their bait shop and boat rental, "Lew's Lively Minnows." Boudreau ran the restaurant while Shotgun took care of the bait shop. He had finally learned the words to *"Jole Blon,"* which made him an honorary Cajun.

Rat

Rudolf Alfons Trommler (Rat) returned to New York and settled in a one-bedroom apartment in Hell's Kitchen. He looked up his old gang. There was only one Blind Duck to be found. The rest were either dead or serving time. The remaining Blind Duck, Pretty Boy, was a homeless drunk. After a year of tending bar, driving a cab, and driving a flower-delivery truck, Rat figured there was a better way, and decided to take advantage of his G.I. Bill benefits. He enrolled in N.Y.U. and got his degree in Business Administration. School came easy for him, so he decided he could do more. He applied for and was accepted into law school. Going to school at night, working days (he had used up his four years' eligibility on the Bill), he got his law degree, passed the bar exam, and became an assistant district attorney in Brooklyn. He was eventually appointed juvenile court judge, trying many teen age gang members. With the advent of the Vietnam War, he would often give the offenders a choice: jail or join the marines. Most opted for jail.

Joe Louis Boyd

Joe returned to Chicago, where he found decent work for a black man was hard to come by. "I appreciate the sacrifice you made for your country, but we're not hiring right now. Come back in a few months."

Finally he said, "Screw this," and started working out at a boxing gym, telling the owner he'd fight anybody, anywhere, anytime. He fought in several illegally staged, unregulated smokers, where he defeated all comers, destroyed most. He was picked up by a manager who got him fights on the under card in New York at Madison Square Garden. He won all of his preliminary fights, and finally, his manager convinced the commission that his boy was ready for a main event fight. On a hot summer night, 1950, Joe climbed into the ring. His opponent was an up-and-coming white boy, Rocky Marciano. Joe was knocked senseless in the first round, knocked out in the second. He returned to Chicago where he found employment as doorman at the Drake Hotel.

Willis

Carl (Governor) Willis made it back to Delaware, returned to college, and got his degree in Political Science. His first job was assistant to the mayor in Dover. The mayor, an aging alcoholic serving his fifth term, liked Willis and was grooming him to take over the office of mayor whenever his liver finally gave out. Willis was encouraged and worked hard. The old man's liver gave out sooner than expected. The new mayor wasn't about to groom Willis to eventually take his job. Instead he gave Willis every crappy assignment that came up. Willis finally quit and ran for City Council. He ran for City Council four times, was never elected, so figured maybe politics wasn't for him after all. His Uncle Ned, who owned a bakery in Wilmington, asked Carl to come work with him, make a small investment, be his partner. This put the fox in the henhouse. Carl put on the weight he had lost, and then some. In a matter of months the only way he could have made it up Nellie's Tit would have been to be pushed in a wheelbarrow.

Plowboy

Edward "Plowboy" Arnold returned to the dairy farm in Pennsylvania, and even though he had sworn he would never milk another cow, he did. For a week. Then he told his dad he was going to go to college. He enrolled at Penn State University, in four years received his degree in agriculture, and had no plans to go back to milking cows. Then something wonderful happened. The automatic milking machine. He and his daddy doubled the size of their herd, and the cows get milked every day. Christmas, Easter Sunday. Even November 10.

Bobby Leeds

After his daring drugstore caper, where his take was three cartons of Lucky Strike cigarettes, Robert (Bobby) Leeds was picked up two days later while trying to rob a bank in Bald Knob Arkansas. Armed only with his finger in the pocket of his jacket, telling the teller it was a gun, the old woman standing in line behind him whopped him in the back of his head with her umbrella. Thus ended the brief criminal career of young Bobby Leeds. He spent three years in the Navy brig for desertion, seven years in the pokey at Hot Springs for the cigarette heist and attemped bank robbery. He returned to Monahans, where he learned that his girl friend, the daughter of the sheriff, wasn't pregnant after all.

Linda Firestone

Linda (Miss Everything) Firestone, immediately following her graduation from McCamey High, moved to California: Hollywood, California, confident that her beauty would take her to the big screen and beyond. The big screen never happened, and the beyond wasn't something to write home about. She worked as a waitress at the Brown Derby, knowing that she would be "discovered." It never happened. She put on weight. Lots of weight. One night while walking home from her cashier's job at Piggly Wiggly, she was attacked by street bum. He showed her his monkey.

The Corpsman's Oath

*I solemnly pledge myself before God
And these witnesses
To practice faithfully
All of my duties as a member of
The hospital corps.
I hold the care of the sick and injured to be a
Sacred trust
And will assist the medical officer
With loyalty and honesty.
I will not knowingly permit harm to come to
Any patient.
I will not partake nor administer
Any unauthorized medication.
I will hold
All personal matters
Pertaining to the private lives of
Patients in strict confidence.
I dedicate my
Heart, mind, and strength
To the work before me.
I shall do all within my power
To show myself an
Example of all that is
Honorable and good
Throughout
My naval career.*